A LANCASTER AMISH HOME FOR JACOB

RACHEL STOLTZFUS

TABLE OF CONTENTS

ACKNOWLEDGMENTS

I have to thank God first and foremost for the gift of my life and the life of my family. I also have to thank my family for putting up with my crazy hours and how stressed out I can get as I approach a deadline. In addition, I must thank the ladies at Global Grafx Press for working with me to help make my books the best they can be. And last, I thank you, for taking the time to read this book. God Bless!

CHAPTER ONE

"Run!" Charles shouted, but Jacob was already running, feet pounding against the broken concrete. He was heading at breakneck speed in the direction of what he knew to be an abandoned building.

Quickly, he grabbed onto a loose drainpipe adjacent to the building's fire escape and began to climb. While others might find this sort of climb incredibly difficult, he always found it fun. The city was full of amazing obstacles, and he loved finding new ways to get around.

On most nights, they were able to do this without so much as a glance from the police, or anyone else for that matter. But on this particular night, Charles had suggested they bring a couple of cans of aerosol paint and work their magic on a car. They had been very proud of their work -- but it did not seem anyone else was, especially the person who called the cops on them.

If they were lucky tonight, very lucky, they might manage

to slip through the unlocked window at the inner-city group home without getting nabbed by the police. If they were even luckier, they might be able to slip into their rooms and into their beds without being noticed. It was more possible than it seemed, actually. They had done it a million times before, though Jacob wished Sherry were with them tonight. She was so much better at planning, strategy and getting out of things.

No sooner were they on the fire escape than they dived through an open window into what they had surmised was an abandoned factory. With any luck, the police outside would simply forget about them. It had happened before. After all, the factory was huge, and as Jacob made his way to the next floor he was not intimidated in the least by the red and blue strobes flashing just beyond the foggy windows. He had been in here a million times before -- maybe a million and one; finding a place to hide was going to be easy.

"Over here!" Charles whispered urgently.

He'd found an old cabinet, lined with grease, but still a decent hiding place. It was better than nothing; that was for sure.

Jacob made a beeline toward the cabinet, following Charles in so that he could close the flimsy metal door behind them.

"Don't close it all the way!" Charles hissed. "If it locks and we die in here, I'm going to kill you!"

Jacob held on to the edge of the door with three fingers,

keeping the gap wide enough to see, but not so wide as to allow anyone to see in.

As he expected, no one came to this floor, but he could hear the sound of metal doors being swung aside and footsteps on the floor below. With any luck, that would be as far as they actually searched.

The footsteps stopped momentarily, and Jacob's heart skipped as the unthinkable happened: they began to come up the stairs.

Jacob and Charlie had both played in this particular factory over the years often enough to know the layout. If the police came up those stairs, they would first encounter a door, and after that door, they would be on what Jacob had always thought to be a factory floor.

There were a million cabinets in here, at least, so the odds of their actually being found were slim to none. But it still made him incredibly nervous. He glanced toward the back of the cabinet, expecting to see Charles, but all he saw was darkness.

"Shh...." Charles said. He was probably placing a finger over his lips.

It was at this moment that Jacob realized there was not nearly enough room in the cabinet for both of them; his legs were at an odd, uncomfortable angle, and he was sure he felt Charles' foot in his bum. In addition to that, he was sure he felt something crawling up his arm. But he dared not move. A single sound could easily give away their position, and the last thing he wanted to do was spend the night in a police station. He'd been there and done that plenty of times.

He thought for a moment at how angry -- or annoyed -- his social worker, Carol would be. She'd be furious if she found out he'd pulled this crap again. Not that it mattered in the end.

The footsteps came nearer, and for the first time Jacob could see light outside of the cabinet.

He squinted, trying to figure out just where that light was coming from while remaining as quiet as possible. Maybe, just maybe, the cops would go away if they didn't hear anything. It was a long shot, though. The cops pretty much never went away on their own.

He gritted his teeth and clenched his fist. They weren't supposed to be here.

At any minute, back at the group home, someone would check their beds, and the 'policy' when one was found empty was to call the police. The home might not have been a jail, but it was the closest thing to it.

Jacob remembered very clearly the last time he'd been in a predicament like this one. He'd been told he was lucky -- extremely lucky -- that the jails were full: otherwise he'd have been occupying his very own 8x4 concrete hotel room.

But Jacob had never been much for threats. And he didn't

consider this much of one.

How much worse could it possibly get? He peeked through the crack once again -- and nearly jumped out of his skin when he saw a pair of blue legs standing right outside the cabinet.

He stopped everything. He stopped moving, stopped looking, stopped *breathing*.

This all seemed very surreal, but in his mind, he was very aware of the situational severity. That was something that had always amused him, actually -- being dragged into the administrator's office after every escapade and being accused of 'not thinking about the consequences of his actions'. That could not be further from the truth. He always thought about the consequences, and was more than aware of them. It was simply that he did not care. And why should he? No one seemed to care about him, after all.

If they did, he'd be living with a family instead of in a crappy group home. Not that he *needed* a family. But in all of his thirteen years, no one had seemed interested in fostering him, and when potential foster parents wandered the halls, he often felt like a dog at the shelter. They didn't take more than a glance at him. He was trouble. He looked like trouble, his file said he was trouble (it was six inches thick, or so he had been told), and the workers at the group home said he was trouble. The truth never seemed to matter -- though the truth was, simply, that he *was* trouble, even if it was only a self-fulfilling prophecy.

Maybe, Jacob thought to himself, just *maybe* the police officer would give up the search and go back to whatever doughnut shop he'd come from, and then, just maybe, he and Charles could sneak back into their room and, for once, be exactly where they were supposed to be in the morning. Turning over a new leaf seemed like the thing to do about now.

As these thoughts raced through his mind, he heard the last thing he ever, *ever* wanted to hear from Charles' mouth:

"Sorry."

Charles had just uttered an actual apology – something that he would never do under normal circumstances.

Suddenly, and without warning beyond that halfhearted apology, Charles kicked him. The force sent him flying out of the cabinet and sprawling across the concrete floor with a yelp.

Immediately, the flashlight beam was on him, and the voice of several police officers echoed throughout the factory floor.

"Freeze! Put your hands on your head!" One of them shouted. Jacob couldn't tell whether they were in a terrible mood or simply excited at the prospect of having something to do. Or both. 'Both' might definitely be worse.

"All right, all right!" Jacob said, rising to his knees and putting his hands on his head.

"I didn't ask to hear your mouth," said the officer, making a beeline for Jacob.

Jacob glanced to his right. Quietly, the cabinet door shut.

"Is there anyone else in here with you?" the officer demanded. He shined the light in nearly every direction, while another officer walked up from behind.

"No," Jacob lied. "It's just me." He was nothing if not loyal.

"You want to tell us what you're doing here?" the officer behind him asked.

Jacob turned to answer, but was grabbed roughly by the first officer.

"Stop moving around!" the officer shouted. "Wait -- I know you. You're that Jacob kid... yeah... The one from the group home."

"You've got me." Jacob shrugged.

"I said I didn't want to hear any of your mouth, and I'm tired of you punk kids thinking you can get away with whatever the hell you want."

"Well, maybe," Jacob said, starting to rise to his feet, "if you'd leave us alone, you wouldn't have to deal with it!"

He knew as the words fell from his mouth that it had been a mistake.

Without warning -- other than Jacob's brief speech -- the officer removed a canister of pepper spray from his belt and delivered a volley directly into Jacob's face.

"I said stop moving!" the officer shouted as Jacob screamed. He fell to his side, assuming the fetal position. He'd been sprayed before, but it didn't exactly get better with time, and he was nowhere near building up an immunity.

His eyes immediately tired up – a futile act on the part of his body to clear the spray from his eyes. Each breath labored, creating the sensation of fire spreading through his throat and nostrils. He tried to scream again, but it caught in his throat, causing not only more pain but a coughing spasm that ended in a stream of vomit surging up from his stomach.

"Oh, well, that's disgusting," the other officer said, kicking Jacob in the back. "You hear that, kid? You're disgusting."

He *hated* the police. They were never helpful or kind like their advertising portrayed: cops were mean, vile creatures with pepper spray, power-mad, with too much time on their hands. When they weren't eating doughnuts and getting fat and lazy, they insisted on chasing nearly-homeless kids like him.

Minutes later, they dragged him from the building, and tossed him into the back of a waiting police car.

Time went by in a blur, and he was booked at the local police station. He was certain he was being questioned, but between the beating and the pepper spray, he couldn't make head or tail of it.

Finally, he heard an officer say something along the lines of "Clearly intoxicated..."

"I'm not drunk," Jacob started to say. But the words once again caught in his throat. He unceremoniously vomited all over the booking counter. Shortly thereafter, he found himself not in a cell, but handcuffed to the handrail at the edge of the lobby.

"Don't want you messin' up one of our cells," the arresting officer said, as he left Jacob practically hanging on the bar.

With nothing left to do, he drifted off into an uncomfortable sleep -- which, if he were very, very lucky, would give the effects of the pepper spray time to wear off. He might even be able to see again.

The least they could do was offer him an eyewash station. But these were cops. Most grownups were useless, but cops were worse than your average grownup. They were useless *and* merciless.

Jacob fell more deeply asleep than he'd wanted. He dreamed of a family picnic, with a mom, dad, two brothers and a dog. It was a dream he had often, but even as he ran across the make-believe lawn, he knew he was dreaming.

His dream parents were kind and rich, and there was a ton of food on the picnic table -- enough to feed everyone in the group home, but all of it for him.

He was jarred awake by a new police officer, one he hadn't seen before. The sight of a new face was not exactly comforting. But at least his eyes no longer burned, and he wasn't cuffed to the railing.

"Kid, wake up," the officer said. "Your social worker's here to pick you up."

Of course she was. Carol wouldn't miss this for the world, would she?

He pulled himself from the floor, utterly exhausted, and took a step forward.

"No, that way." The officer corrected him, turning him in the right direction.

The first thing Jacob noticed was that the world beyond the plate-glass windows at the front of the station had transitioned from night to early morning, with the bright Pennsylvania sun assaulting nearly all of the senses he had left after last night. This place could really do with some blinds, he thought.

The second thing he noticed was Carol, his Social Worker. She was standing in the doorway, wearing her usual white turtleneck and toting that huge pleather bag. She looked angry, but that was nothing new.

He walked toward her.

He was not afraid of her, per se, but when she wanted to, she could have a serious temper. He was expecting her to read him the riot act. In fact, he almost expected to be smacked in the back of the head a few times during the ride back, and told how much of an idiot he was, how he made her life hard and how she didn't like a hard life. He expected the usual threats: you will be tied to your bed; your food privileges will be cut; blah, blah, blah.

She was not a half-bad caseworker. He'd had worse. She did seemed to genuinely care about him – at least, as much as time allowed, with her caseload of fifty-three other rejects and losers like him.

This time she made no threats, just looked at him sadly, and that made him nervous.

Disappointment, that was her look, as her eyes seemed to bore a shaft straight into his soul. It wasn't a new thing, of course. She was all of fifty years old, which, when held in comparison to Jacob's mere thirteen years on the planet, seemed like an eternal gap that would never be traversed. She'd been on the job far too long, and, deep down, Jacob realized that his crap was the probably the straw that was breaking her back. How many times in the last month had he been in trouble?

While he felt some remorse for the hell he put her through, he only had enough room in his mind to worry about himself, and what was coming next.

"Let's go," she said, turning to the door and walking briskly through the airlock, onto the street. A cold blast of air hit Jacob as he followed her, eventually reaching the sidewalk and her waiting car.

He had no idea what time it was, but with the sun barely creeping over the tops of the buildings, he guessed that it was still well before eight in the morning.

They both climbed into the car -- an old Cavalier, all that Carol could afford on her meager salary. He figured the only thing going through her mind on the way back to the group home was: *"I really do not get paid enough for this."*

The ride back to the home was short, and even shorter than usual due to the lack of traffic on the city streets. Carol pulled her car into the parking lot located behind the building, purposefully ignoring the speed bump placed at the entrance. Jacob's head hit the roof of the car. He shot Carol a dirty look.

"Then wear your seat belt," she said sharply in response to his unspoken criticism as she pulled into one of the free parking spaces. "Get out."

He complied, if only to avoid her wrath.

Carol purposefully made tracks across the parking lot, likely to avoid talking to Jacob before she had to. One could hardly blame her, but Jacob had a hard time keeping up.

Moments later they were sitting in her makeshift office. It had been erected years ago using cubicle dividers in the corner beside an exterior door. In fact, the 'walls' were not nearly tall enough to provide any sort of privacy, and the door to the office was a re-purposed door from inside the group home. He couldn't remember where the door had come from, and neither could anyone else. All that mattered, he had come to understand, was that the state did not have to pay for it, and that made it a good thing.

Carol sat behind her desk, shuffling through papers as she often did. Jacob often wondered what type of degree she had to have for such a mundane job. But his thoughts were interrupted as she finally dropped the papers, and stared across the desk at him.

"I'm going to be frank," she said, in a freakishly monotone voice. "What the hell? I mean, really. What the hell?"

This was a bit terrifying. He had never heard Carol curse.

"Okay," said Carol, "listen. We have our limits – well, the limits the state imposes on us. The fact is, Jacob, we can't--"

Carol's speech was rudely interrupted by a knock on the cubicle door. In this universe, knocking granted an individual permission to simply enter the office, as Carrie, the other social worker, now did. She did that half-in half-out thing that Jacob found utterly annoying as she spoke.

"Hiiii," she said, stretching out her word, as if it was going to make the interruption any less annoying. As she spoke, she constantly smacked her lips, apparently a side effect of trying to enunciate her words. "I just wanted to let you know that...Mack...the one upstairs...he made poo-poo on the floor--"

"Get out," Carol said flatly.

"I'm sorry?" Carrie said, looking offended.

"I said get out. Close the door behind you."

As soon as the door closed, Carol continued her impromptu speech. "Bottom line," she said, "you can't stay here anymore."

"Is this supposed to be bad news?" Jacob asked, slouching down in the chair.

"It *is* bad news," Carol said. "There are only a few other places open, one of them being a mental hospital on the south side. Of course, considering your actions last night, you're more likely to spend time in juvenile detention."

"Or I could take my chances on the streets," Jacob suggested. "I never asked for your help." That old rage began to well within him, as he felt his stomach constrict and his throat tighten, and he burned to pound his fist on something or somebody. "You could have just let me die back then."

"You couldn't go for one night without being picked up by the police," Carol pointed out. "How do you think you're going to do out there?"

"I could do it," Jacob insisted. The fact that 'back then' had been when he was a baby made little difference. He was now on the brink of manhood. Everyone told him that, to try to make him comply with this or that. Until right now, he hadn't figured a way to work that expression to his favor. Until now.

"No, you couldn't," Carol said, no longer bothering to look

up from her paperwork. Her shoulders were slouched – rolled, he thought; that sight you see in older adults or people exhausted or depressed. He guessed she might be all of those right now.

Finally, she spoke. "You're an idiot."

"I'm not an idiot," Jacob muttered, sinking further into the chair. "Whatever you say," Carol said. "Now there are some other options . . . well, one other option. I can't get you a foster family in the city; quite frankly, you're considered a sociopath, and those foster families have a right to know that an idiotic, psycho like you would be coming to live with them."

"They don't even know me," Jacob quietly protested.

"I don't care; you're going to be labeled a sociopath. Especially after what you told the State psychiatrist," Carol said, still reading her paperwork.

"I was joking. I fed her all the lines from a kid on 'Law & Order.' It wasn't real."

"Well, she took it to be real. That's why I called you an idiot. *I* know you're not psycho, but it's becoming increasing difficult for me to convince others of that fact.

"There's a family outside the city that owes me a favor," she went on. "It might be just what you need -- a fresh start, a place where you can live, learn and grow into adulthood as a good citizen. Honestly, I think the city places are simply a revolving door to nowhere. At least this way, you'll have a chance at a decent life. It won't be easy, but it'll keep you out of jail and off the streets. And that's what counts. I know you don't believe anyone cares for you," she wound up, "but I do. And, this might be a chance for you to pull your life together."

Jacob blinked, but didn't reply. In fact, he didn't know what to say. In those few words, she had summed up his life with her – *messed-up* – and offered to give him a chance to start over . . . because she... cared about him.

That last part was hard to fathom; it had been so long since anyone had expressed anything toward him that he felt his stomach constrict. Only Charles and Sherry were even slightly close, and even they never flat-out came and told him they cared about him.

He shook his head and forced himself back to the present. He thought about the other thing she had said: She was sending him to "the country."

When that hit him, he just stared at her. *I didn't know Pennsylvania had a country,* he thought.

"Outside the city? Where outside the city?" he said finally.

The idea of actually leaving the city kind of appealed to him, though he was always a little apprehensive about leaving Charles and Sherry behind. Then again, they were like family. They always found their way back to one another, somehow.

"Far outside. I'm not even sure if you'll even have a zip code. But it beats the alternative." Carol pushed her graying hair back from her eyes, and stared at him with her tired blue-eyed gaze. "You are a pain in the ass, because you're smart," she said. "I know life has dealt you a lousy hand; I cannot change that. But I want to give you a chance. And calling in this favor might be the only thing left."

Outside the cubicle, Jacob could hear the day starting. The outer door was constantly opening, with that horrid squeaking noise accompanied by the shuffling of footsteps and the low, murmuring voices that came standard with group home workers this early in the morning. It had become clear to Jacob long ago that none of them actually wanted to be here, and, for the life of him, he couldn't figure out why they didn't simply seek employment elsewhere.

After all, they were always telling him that he could be anything he wanted, if he just put his mind to it. It never went over well when he turned it around by saying, "Then why aren't you a millionaire?" or "Then why don't you have that pilot's license you always talk about?"

It had occurred to him long ago that maybe, just maybe, life wasn't as full of sunshine and flowers as they were trying to lead him to believe. In spite of that, he stayed at the group home under both mandate of law, and the promise of three meals per day and a bed -- even if the meals weren't always hot and the bed was pretty uncomfortable.

"The alternative being jail, right?" Jacob said. His eyes wandering to the walls of the 'office'. He realized idly that

Carol had all these fake pictures on the wall: framed representations of happy children in fake families, little girls in pretty sundresses and boys running through meadows laughing. She also had kid stuff: pictures of cartoon characters that might have entertained children half his age.

"Or the psych ward," Carol agreed. "There just aren't enough beds. And, to be frank, there are kids out there who want that bed more than you do."

He didn't answer, but instead continued to survey the walls of the cubicle. It was such a – he didn't have a word to describe it – but it meant roughly that what was on the walls seldom matched the reality of life. He'd also heard this speech a million times before, although, to be honest, he'd never actually been kicked out of the group home.

"Do you have anything to say? Any input at all?" Carol asked. Her tone was becoming less patient.

Jacob shrugged and kept staring at the walls. He'd fixated on what appeared to be a makeshift calendar Carol had made. He wondered if he should express some emotion, but it would probably be as fake as the pictures on her walls. In reality, he didn't care that much about his fate: group home or foster home, it was pretty much all the same to him.

"Fine," Carol said finally. "Get upstairs, pack your stuff, and get back down here. Someone will be around to pick you up in a bit. Best you say goodbye to your friends... No, scratch that; you haven't made any friends here. With the exception of

Charles, who may be following you to the country."

Jacob silently pushed the chair out, stood up, and walked toward the cubicle door.

Passing a mirror, he was struck by how small he looked. Stringy hair pasted to his forehead, daiquiri-blue eyes dulled by neglect and want looking back at him; slightly hunched shoulders, rolled over by the weight of his situation, he guessed. It was not a pretty picture, and from the image in that mirror, he thought he might have shrunk. Was he really getting shorter?

He half-shrugged to himself, accepting the situation. His mouth was downturned, and there were dark circles and redness around his tired gaze; they were a holdover from the pepper spray. Maybe that was why he seemed shorter today, too.

"Jacob, push the chair in," Carol said. As usual, he ignored her, and simply exited without turning around, squeezing through the door, as wide as it would open with the chair sitting in the way.

It was a juvenile kind of resistance, he knew. Nevertheless, what else did he have? No family, few friends, a foster care system that couldn't give a fig about him… and now he was nearly homeless.

Oh, yeah, and he was a sociopath, whatever the heck that was. He had accomplished all this after being on this lousy planet for only 4789 days.

But Carol, who always came and picked him up from whatever trouble he got himself into, was now giving him a chance. Maybe, he thought, with a little flash of surprise, it wouldn't have been too much to push the chair in.

He took the stairs up to the second floor of the home. Surprisingly enough, it was clean this morning. He found the door to his room, swung it open, and walked in to find Charles lying in his bed.

"Welcome back," Jacob said, walking straight past him.

"Don't know what you're talking about," Charles said smugly. "I've been here all night."

"I hope you can get used to being alone for a while," Jacob said. "They're shipping me out to the middle of nowhere."

He knew he should be angry with Charles, but he couldn't be. He knew that Charles' leg had nearly cramped off, back there in the cabinet, had been a matter of throwing him under the bus or screaming bloody murder. He understood the rationale: Why should they both have gotten caught?

"It won't last long," Charles said with a laugh. "We always end up back here."

"Not this time," Jacob said as he stuffed his clothes into a small duffel bag. He went to the doorway and turned back around. "You know, you owe me one," he said.

He looked at Charles for a moment longer. Even though they were best friends, he didn't feel a hug was in order. That would be too much like connecting, and he didn't like to connect to people. You just got disappointed in the end. "See you around," he said.

"That's right, keep your hopes up!" Charles called after him as he made his way down the hall. "There's always emancipation. Then we can live where we want."

It was a familiar refrain, shouted between two foster kids whose biggest hope was to finally become adults and leave the system, or to get old enough to ask for emancipation and get out on their own. Two fifteen-year-olds in their group home had done it, and had left all happy, like they'd won the lottery. Conquering heroes who'd left to make something of themselves in the big, bad world.

Jacob had seen them a couple of times afterwards, walking down the streets looking like they were on top of the world. He'd asked how they were doing, and they'd said great, fantastic, working at McDonalds was a career path to fame and fortune. He hadn't believed it, but he'd wished them well and played along.

In reality, they'd both looked a little hungry.

"Long live King Emancipation!" he called back, as he headed down the stairs. He wasn't headed to a life of splendor at McDonalds, but he was going to a place that might be far worse – the country.

Why did the thought of the wilds of Pennsylvania fill him with so much anger, and so much dread? Well, no matter what happened, the other group-homers and the social workers weren't going to see how scared he was. He sauntered toward the office, to sit and wait for his ride.

***

"We've been driving for hours," Jacob complained. "I haven't seen a building in...well...hours. Where *are* we?"

"Don't ask me, kid," said the driver. "I just get paid to take people here...well, there...wherever 'here' is. You know."

"Have you ever brought anyone out this far before?" Jacob asked, genuinely curious.

"Ah, no, actually . . . and I hope they pay me a little better for this one."

Another two hours dragged on. Jacob was beginning to wonder if he would ever see the highway again.

Finally, they passed a green township sign that simply read: "Hope Crossing".

It was an old sign, and the poles supporting it were bent, as if they'd been hit, toppled, and re-erected dozens of time. After the sign came a long stretch of road, a few farmhouses here and there, and then finally, for the first time in hours, a town.

A real town! Jacob sat up in his seat, trying to catch a

glimpse of this place called 'Hope Crossing.' But he realized almost immediately that it would be nothing like the city. There were a few cars parked here and there, but what really drew his attention were the horse-drawn buggies. They were everywhere, and he could see some of the most strangely dressed people walking up and down the sidewalk. They almost looked like . . . could that really be right? . . . Pilgrims.

"Where *are* we?" Jacob asked the driver. "Did we go back in time?"

"I hit 85 a while back," the driver said with a straight face. "But no, seriously, this place is called Hope Crossing. It's an Amish community. Old backward folk, if you ask me."

"'Backward'?" Was he going to live with a bunch of idiots?

"Well, look around you, kid. They ride in buggies when there are perfectly good cars. They don't even have electricity."

"That's crap. I saw a light on in that store," Jacob pointed to a grocery store that was proudly advertising 'Amish Whoopie Pies' in the window.

"Those stores are owned by normal folk... probably not something you'll be seeing for a while."

"What do you mean?" said Jacob suspiciously.

"From what I hear, you did some nasty stuff back in the city. Ms. Carol pulled some strings to keep you out of jail, and she does not want you anywhere near the home -- or near any buildings over three stories tall, for that matter. You're going to live with the Amish."

"The people with no electricity?!"

Great. No video games, no television, no radio. Ms. Carol sure knew how to punish a person. Dropped in the middle of nowhere with nothing -- with less than nothing.

Come to think of it, it was kind of fitting for him, because he was worth less than nothing.

"And I get paid to deliver you to the gates of hell." The driver chuckled. "Isn't it great how that works?"

"Absolutely fantastic," said Jacob.

They drove for still another twenty minutes: down the road, flanked by massive fields, long fences, and kinds of livestock that he'd heard about in school, but had never actually seen before.

"I'm so screwed," he muttered, low enough that he thought the driver wouldn't hear.

"Yep," the driver answered calmly, as he took a left turn into what must have passed for a driveway around here.

In fact, it looked less like a driveway than like a long, winding gravel path that someone had laid down haphazardly. Jacob briefly wondered if they would not have been better off with a dirt road. Maybe it would have been less bumpy.

They were heading toward a farmhouse, a large one, though it was dwarfed by the outline of the barn behind it. Jacob briefly wondered if these people were farmers. But his thought process was interrupted by the vehicle coming to a stop, and then by the appearance of what Jacob could only assume was an Amish man on the porch of the house.

The driver stepped out of the vehicle, and Jacob followed. Moments later, the driver was handing the man a piece of paper. "I need you to sign here, or I don't get paid," he said.

The man put pen to paper and handed it back. Then he stood waiting for the driver to turn the vehicle around and exit his property.

Jacob looked at the Amish man who had emerged from the house. This was, easily, the largest man he had ever seen. The guy stood six feet tall at least, and wore clothes that looked as if they'd come directly from the 18th century.

Despite his strange manner of dress, he was intimidating – more so than Jacob had ever seen in any other man. And, of course, Jacob still had that little shrinking problem from the pepper spray, so he felt even shorter than usual. It was like staring up at a tree with a hat on top.

"My name is Thomas," the man said. He towered over Jacob like a skyscraper. "Thomas Mast.

"I know all about you, Jacob," he went on. "There will be no shenanigans here. You will not find any cars to spray paint;

you will not disturb our way of life. Look to your left, look to your right. Look behind you. There is no city; there are no houses, and hardly any people. Nowhere for you to go. But," he added, "if you should find that this place does not appeal to you, you are free to take your bag and your two legs, and walk off in the direction that tickles your fancy."

Jacob just stared up at him, dumbstruck. The man went on:

"If you stay, you can expect to be treated like a member of my family, with all the rules and consequences that entails. You will have an opportunity to earn our trust, respect and affection. That last part is entirely up to you. Right now, you have no black marks against you. See to it that you keep it that way or suffer the consequences of transgression. I hope we're clear on that point."

Thomas Mast stared at him for a moment to see if his point was made. Then he turned toward the house. Jacob was sure he felt the man's steps shaking the Earth as he walked. He vanished into the house as if he'd been a giant apparition, some large -- no, massive -- white tree-ghost in a straw hat, farmer's clothes and a long beard.

This had to be a joke. Suffer the consequences of transgression? That didn't sound too good.

Jacob was put in mind of those old prison movies he had seen at the group home, when the tough guy first met the warden. The warden made a speech; the tough guy listened and then when the warden was finished, he turned and left the prisoner to be led away to his cell. All this place lacked was a black-and

-white background, and a six-by-nine cell with loud clanking bars.

"I should have gone to the psych ward and taken the drugs they give sociopaths," Jacob murmured to himself.

He stood there staring at the closed door, wondering if he should try to get across the porch. Then he made a decision and tiptoed across the wooden planks toward the door.

"Mr. Mast... uh... Thomas?" What did he do now?

Clearly, the man had taken him in under duress. And he had made it clear that if Jacob walked away, he would be on his own. The flip side to that was that if he stayed, he would be treated like a Mast... whatever that meant.

It didn't sound too much different from being treated like a sociopath. Both treatments were unknown, probably dreadful, and therefore similar.

This was certainly different from the group home. Mr. Thomas- the-Tree-with-a-Straw-Hat Mast did not even make a pretense of caring for him. He *had* said that Jacob had the opportunity to earn it. The group home hung up signs saying how much they cared, which were there no matter what he did . . . and it was all a lie.

At least, here, he knew where he stood: he was dirt under

his host's shoe. He had a chance to earn more than that -- but he also had a chance to suffer consequences. Which sounded a lot like the hammer of doom, coming down from Thor, complete with ground- splitting and lightning strikes.

CHAPTER TWO

As the self-absorbed driver from child services had predicted, Jacob had landed in some sort of Pilgrim nightmare.

The Mast family lived on what Jacob had at first assumed to be a farm. But, as it turned out, not all Pilgrims were farmers -- contrary to popular belief and his own small amount of knowledge.

Before being shown to his room, Jacob had been informed by a woman named Dorothy that the Mast family (if you could consider this a family) ran some sort of furniture business, and that he would be helping them with it. It didn't exactly sound like a request.

Regardless, he didn't feel like arguing. In fact, he was extremely tired after the long car ride, and more than happy to make his way to bed.

Dorothy -- a woman old enough to be his mother -- had shown him to an upstairs room and shut the door behind him.

The room was small, but larger than what he had shared at the group home. And in this room the walls were actually intact. Imagine that! No bullet holes, no holes where temper had gotten the better of a person.

There was absolutely nothing in this room aside from a small bed, a table, and what Jacob assumed was a lamp. There was also a Bible in the table drawer, along with a notebook and a pencil.

Closer inspection revealed the lamp-like object was a battery-operated lantern, the type you would find in the camping section of a hardware store. Apparently, these people did have light when it suited them. His original assessment of everyone standing around in the dark after sunset had been wrong. But right now, he didn't care if they ran naked through the forest dancing in the moonlight. He was exhausted and further examination of his room was not worth the effort. He turned the battery lamp on and looked at the bed.

It was the best bed he had ever seen.

Jacob collapsed onto the bed without touching the light, and soon enough found himself drifting off into his own personal dreamland. As usual, his dreams were an incoherent pile of nonsensical and nightmarish images. Some had to do with the group home, and its tattered walls. Others were about his make-believe family, smiling and offering him fried chicken, mashed potatoes, string beans, corn bread and cake. Lots to drink, endless soda cups, and a mom who hugged him and called him "my Jacob".

He also dreamed of Sherry, the red-haired girl he'd met so long ago -- at least from his perspective. From the days of kicking her on the playground, to the secret kiss he'd stolen from her in the group home closet on the third floor – the floor he was never supposed to access, but did anyway. Because of Sherry, he'd spent a considerable amount of time there.

His memories had faded over time. But Sherry -- she was the one constant that he could always hold clear as crystal in his mind's eye. She was beautiful, with red hair, green eyes, and a shy smile that made him feel warm right down to his toes.

In another environment, she might have been the popular girl at school, or maybe even a movie star. Who knew? In any case, she was nice to him, like a sister; and, as time passed, a friend with benefits. The group home janitor had taught him that phrase, although he figured the janitor's friends did a lot more than steal kisses in a closet. He had seen a couple of them; skanks by any measure, who had toyed with him and then cast him aside for a real man.

His dreams of Sherry made Jacob feel whole. She was the one thing he would miss about the group home. All the rest of his dreams, he could take with him.

His dream was the same as it always was, at least when it involved Sherry. She was at the end of the third-floor hallways, near the second set of stairs. He was running toward her, but with each step, the corridor seemed to become longer, and longer, and longer. She was calling out to him, but he couldn't hear her. He ran, and ran, and ran, never seeming to close the gap between them, and finally, just when it seemed he might be making some progress, he was, as always, woken up.

"Wake up!" Thomas Mast practically shouted. He was shaking Jacob's shoulder hard. "It's time to work!"

Slowly and deliberately, Jacob opened his eyes.

The room was pitch black, something he hadn't expected. The only light came from the electric lantern beside his bed, which was now dimmed from his neglecting to shut it off before he'd lain down. Wonderful.

"Wake up, and bring that lantern with you!" The tree had spoken.

Thomas Mast left the room, and Jacob was left to drag himself from the bed. His eyes weighed a million and a half pounds, and his body simply did not want to respond. Who in their right mind would get up this early?

He stumbled across the room and peered out the window. As he suspected, it was still dark; the only light was provided by the moon.

He shook his head and made up his mind. What could it hurt to go back to bed for a few more minutes? He walked back across the room and collapsed back into the bed. "Just ten more minutes," he mumbled to himself.

He wasn't sure if he dreamed during those ten minutes, but he was sure that he was rudely awakened much sooner than he would have liked. This time, instead of a rough shake on the shoulder, he was doused with a bucket of cold water. It enveloped his entire body, and caused him to wake with a start.

"What the hell?!" he demanded, sitting straight up, his entire body tensed on high alert. He leapt from the bed, looking about, and then wiped his eyes.

There in front of him stood a girl about his own age, dressed in the 'pilgrim clothes' that he'd seen in town earlier.

"That's a naughty word. If you curse around daed, you'll get punished," she said, without the slightest hint of humor. "Breakfast will be ready in five minutes."

Jacob collapsed onto the bed again. Breakfast? Who got 'breakfast' ready in the morning? Hadn't these people heard of Pop Tarts?

He closed his eyes for a moment, but was rudely interrupted by another splash of water.

"That one had soap in it. For dirty words," the girl said as she left the room. She reminded him of an elf: curly blond hair, bright smile, plain clothes, good shoes -- and that stupid bucket of water. An elf on meth.

"I'm awake!" Jacob shouted. "You don't have to keep doing that!"

He finally rose from the bed, looking about. On a chair near the door was a set of clothing, close to his size. But it was the 'Amish' clothing he was already learning to despise. A dress-up shirt, suspenders, and slacks. No buttons, just hooks. Didn't these people believe in belts?

Feeling rather annoyed, he stripped his clothes off, and replaced them with the clothes that had been left for him.

Instead of tennis shoes like he was used to, he had been given a pair of leather work boots -- and to top it off, they had been previously worn. In fact, he could swear that some parts of these boots were thinner than others. It was just as well, he'd never been given anything new in his life. He pulled them onto his feet, lacing them up, and stumbled out of the bedroom, now more or less awake. The boots weighed heavily on his feet. He looked back longingly at his sneakers once before he clopped toward the staircase.

He managed to find a bathroom near the middle of the hallway. To his relief, the house was actually stocked with typical bathroom supplies, though they could have sprung for a pump soap. Well, beggars can't be choosy.

When he'd finished, he clopped on off down the stairs, and into the kitchen.

At first, he thought he had arrived in food heaven. There were scrambled eggs, meats, biscuits, and milk or tea to drink. He hadn't seen so much food in one place since… well, he had never seen this much food. As well, everyone was taking food, not snatching it, and quiet pleasantries were being exchanged.

It was definitely different from the group home, where you had to fight for what you got, and usually lost half of it to the older kids anyway. Here, in fact, no one seemed interested in much of anything, as he slid into what he assumed would be his chair at the table.

There was already a plate of food in front of him, containing a few pieces of bacon, eggs, and a biscuit, plus a glass of milk. He was torn between eating slowly, licking his lips and savoring each bite, and eating as fast as possible, stuffing food in his mouth quickly. The latter won out, and he stuffed his face.

Mr. Mast was to his right, and Jacob felt his monstrous, tree-like branch touch his hand.

"No one will take the food, boy," he said quietly.

He then returned to eating, as Jacob stared at him, mouth slightly open.

Jacob looked around the table. Everyone continued eating as if nothing had just transpired.

Jacob slowed down just a little, eyeing his new family as he ate. The only sounds throughout the kitchen were those of knives and forks, clanking against the ceramic plates.

The silence was strange: At the group home, there was clanging, clatter and chatter through the meal. Jacob hunched over the food, protecting it from sudden departure, despite Thomas Mast's words.

He had eaten no more than half his plate before Thomas Mast rose from the table. His head nearly struck the ceiling as he did.

"We're off," he said, in his quiet, yet booming, voice. He pointed at Jacob.

"I'm not done..." he began to say, and the girl sitting across from him giggled. He wanted more food; he wasn't finished. Was this going to be how they stole from him?

Thomas was already walking toward the back door. He stopped and looked back, waiting. Jacob stared at his half-empty plate, then back at the Mast-tree.

"You'd better be off," the older woman, Dorothy, said gently. She handed him a couple of biscuits with bacon and eggs, wrapped in a napkin. "We've still got plenty of water." She smiled at him.

Jacob slid his chair back and began to run for the back door. Great, he was thinking: here you get a lot of food, but not enough time to eat it. Either way, starvation.

"Push it in," Dorothy called after him.

What was it with people and chairs? All that ever happened was you had to pull it back out again later on. Total waste of energy, as far as he was concerned. *I swear,* he thought to himself as he ran back to push the chair in, *I'll never sneak out of the home again. And no more papier-mâché pranks -- never, ever again.*

He ran after the Amish warden, grabbing the straw hat and dumping his food in it as he ran. Well, at least the woman had given him more food. But he was running so fast that he didn't have time to eat it. He shoved a piece of the bacon into his mouth and continued to hurry behind Mr. Mast.

***

They were not giving him much time to get settled in, that was for sure.

As soon as they approached a barn, Thomas directed him to a wooden cart that looked as if it had been pulled directly from an old John Wayne movie and motioned for him to sit in the back.

"Don't sit on the edge," Thomas warned, as he took the bench seat in the front, tending to the horses that he had already hitched. "You'll fall off, and I don't have time to come find you. Storm's coming. Finish your breakfast. I don't need you hungry."

"How the hell do you know when it's going to rain?" Jacob said, almost mockingly. "You don't have TV."

"I trust the good Lord to tell me. And we don't curse in this family." Thomas signaled the horses to move forward, nearly knocking Jacob out of the cart. It was difficult for Jacob to tell whether he was joking or not. He sure wished the 'good Lord' would give him a hand at staying inside the cart while it was on the move. How was he supposed to eat and hang on at the same time?

The sky was beginning to lighten, with the slightest hint of blue creeping into what had once been a beautiful starlit canvas. Though it might be hard to believe -- as it always was -- the sky would soon be alight under a blazing sun. Although Thomas seemed to believe that it would be gray and wet. Good evidence that the man was clearly insane.

As a result of Thomas's paranoia, they arrived at their destination faster than Jacob had expected -- their destination being a patch of forest located directly on the Mast property, though it was far enough out that Jacob could not see the ancient farmhouse in the distance.

As Jacob climbed out of the cart, Thomas walked by him without a word and handed him an old ax. For a moment, Jacob was shocked. At the group home, there was a strict no-weapons policy; anyone caught with so much as a pocketknife was subject to prosecution. In fact, Jacob had begun to wonder if they didn't just enjoy the idea of shipping people off to the county jail.

"What am I supposed to do with this?" Jacob asked, holding his hat full of food in one hand and the ax in the other. He made a quick decision, stuffed a biscuit in his mouth, and started to place the hat in the back of the wagon.

Thomas Mast looked at him. He shook his head. "Why do you eat so slowly?"

Jacob felt a sarcastic answer swelling to the surface of his mind, but squelched it for the truth.

"I've never had this much good food that I wasn't fighting over," he said. He stuffed more of the biscuit in his mouth.

Once again, he felt the tree branch on his shoulder.

"I will wait, but be quick about it." Thomas turned away from him once again, looking at the sky.

What was he seeing that Jacob didn't? It looked like a perfect day to him.

Jacob gulped down the last of his breakfast, shook out his hat, stuffed the cloth napkin in his hat and stuck it on his head. "I'm ready," he said.

Jacob walked up beside the Mast-tree, looking in the same direction he was. Mr. Mast handed him the ax, adjusted his hat so the sun wasn't in his eyes, and started off.

"Follow me," he said behind him to Jacob, as he headed into the forest. "I need timber for the shop, but I don't want wet timber. We're going to fill the cart up and get back before the storm starts up."

"Fine," Jacob said, and followed Thomas into the forest.

He would not say it aloud, but he briefly wondered why Thomas would need an ax to cut down a tree. The man was the size of a grizzly bear, and looked as if he could tear a building down with his bare hands.

This thought quickly fled from his mind as he became aware of the length of their 'hike' into the forest. It wasn't long before his feet began to ache and his legs turned to rubber. It wasn't that he'd never walked this far before -- but the terrain was so different! Jacob had never walked this far uphill in his entire life. And to top it all off, someone (Thomas) had been kind enough to awaken him long before dawn.

"I need to stop," Jacob said, resting against the ax handle. "No time," Thomas snapped. "Storm's coming."

Jacob peered up, through the canopy of trees, which now gave way to a light blue sky. He couldn't see a single cloud. What he could see were a few stars – stragglers from the night before, or what the sky leaves behind when it's tired and wants to move on to the next thing.

Thomas was already moving along, deeper into the forest. That gave Jacob no choice but to follow him into the trees, the ax dragging behind him on the damp forest floor.

"Here," Thomas said, pointing to a tree. "Cut that down. From this side."

Jacob felt as if his body were going to fall apart at any moment, but he was in no mood or condition to argue. Under the watchful eye of Thomas, he took up his position in front of the tree, and took a swing at the trunk.

The ax barely dented the bark, and Jacob felt an indescribable pain shoot through his shoulders in response. He immediately dropped the ax and stared at his hands.

It felt as if his skin had been torn, and he expected to find blood. But there was nothing – nothing but the ax being shoved back into his hands by Thomas.

"I won't abide you slacking," Thomas said. "Put your hands apart, one at the bottom, one in the middle. Put your body into it, and take that tree down!"

Jacob once again gripped the ax, as told, and took a swing. But he got no further into it this time than he had the last time. In fact, the ax actually bounced off the trunk, and would have hit Thomas, had he not been standing a good four feet away.

"Pathetic," Thomas said. "Englischers! Good for nothing, they told me; good for nothing you are. Step aside."

"No," Jacob said, feeling anger rise up within him. He felt that old rage building inside of him, that feeling he got whenever people pushed him aside.

Thomas said nothing as Jacob prepared to swing the ax again. Instead, he simply reached in front of him and snatched the tool from his hands, pushing Jacob out of the way and sending him sprawling across the forest floor.

"Hey!" Jacob shouted. "I could be good for something if you showed me. You can't call me good for nothing and a slacker just because I don't know how to cut down a tree. I've never *held* an ax."

He realized his fists were balled, and he consciously loosened them.

Mast regarded him for a moment, his eyes slightly squinted, eyebrows furrowed.

"All right," he said. "I'll show you how to do this. Then you do it. Then we leave. Fair?"

Thomas took up his own ax, and took a mighty swing at the tree. The first hit took the blade at least an inch into the tree, which was no more than three inches around anyway. The next hit nearly took the tree down.

He was about to strike it with the ax again, but then he stopped. "You do it," he said. "Right here." He pointed at the wedge he had just made.

Jacob took the ax, held it the way he had seen Mast hold it, took aim and swung.

The ax barely made contact with the tree, and Jacob realized that Mr. Mast had left it almost ready to fall over. All he needed to do, really, was push it, and it would have fallen. But he had given Jacob the chance to finish the job.

As the tree started to fall, it gave off a deafening crack and the towering tree fell away from them, onto the forest floor.

Jacob spun around, a large grin on his face. What would they think back at the group home? Good food, and he had just chopped down a tree!

Well, he'd *almost* chopped it down.

He was beginning to like the Mast-tree man, just a little.

"I forgot the saw back at the cart," said Mr. Mast. "Run back there and grab it. Then come cut the top off of this tree." Mr. Mast started working on the smaller branches with the ax.

Again? Jacob thought. It was like with the food: everyone acted as if nothing had happened.

The Amish were a strange lot. But he was beginning to have a bit of hope that he might be able to stay here. It was still only the first day, though; no need to go getting hopes up only to have them knocked down, like they always were.

Despite what Mast had said, there was no 'running' to be done as he went back to the cart: every part of Jacob's body ached, and he was certain it would be worse by tomorrow.

Jacob had always done most of his walking through alleys and urine, among rat-infested buildings. It was flat land, stinking and foul. It didn't take as much effort as it took to walk up and down hills.

He made his way across this rolling terrain back to the cart limping and moaning all the way, stopping periodically to rest against a tree. It took at least fifteen minutes – or, from his perspective, several hours -- but he finally made it to the edge of the tree line, and to the waiting cart in the open field. It took a few seconds, but he was finally able to locate the handsaw, which was -- no exaggeration -- almost as long as he was.

"Holy crap," he muttered. "How do I carry this thing?"

He wound up dragging it back up through the forest. He didn't want to get sawed up if he fell, so he pulled   it behind him. It felt heavier and heavier as he climbed, moving as fast as he could without tripping and falling.

With any luck, he thought, he'd run into Thomas, but luck aside, what was more than likely was that he'd get lost. Not that he was a pessimist; he should be feeling happy he'd knocked down a tree. But all this moving and hauling was taking its toll on him. As he clopped along, he hoped the path back it was a straight shot into the woods – or, anyway, that it would have been if he didn't have to keep stopping to catch his breath every three feet.

There were many things in life Jacob wanted, but right now, more than anything, he wanted to take these worn leather boots off and rub his feet. That was one wish he'd never had before. He was beginning to understand why Carol was always talking about 'getting off her feet'. She was small and thin -- probably because she was always running after some kid or another -- but when she sat down in her office, she always pulled her feet halfway out of her black pumps. It was the only time she got any rest. And now, clopping along in these leather boots, Jacob thought he had a better understanding of why she did that.

He arrived back at the work site, to his relief. There he found that several trees already felled, all of them piled nice and neat in a straight line. Five of them, to be exact.

"Cut the tops off!" Mr. Mast yelled from somewhere within the forest.

Jacob looked, but couldn't seem him through the trees -- which he thought was kind of funny, because the man was as tall as a tree, with hair the color of sunlight. Not exactly someone who blended in. But somehow, right now, he did.

Jacob moved toward the pile of trees. He took up the saw and attempted to saw through the tops of the trees – in order, he assumed, to get rid of the branches.

"Cut higher!" yelled the voice.

"How can you even see me?" Jacob muttered as he sawed in vain at the tops of the fallen trees.

He managed to cut through two, but as he started on the third, Thomas appeared out of nowhere to grab the other end of the saw and. They started a twosome sawing exercise that got them through all five trees in short order.

"You have school now, boy," Thomas said, as Jacob rubbed his abraded hands and wiped his sweat. "The state says you have to go, or I'd work you all day. You need to learn a lot, and

I am willing to teach you. You've done well for someone who never held an ax before. I'll cut the trees until you get the hang of it, and you'll cut off the tops. But you must also go to school. That's the law, and my promise to your social worker."

"I'm not finished," Jacob said angrily, reaching for the saw again.

Normally, he wouldn't have cared. There was nothing quite as satisfying getting out of a chore. But this Thomas Mast-tree man had made him angry – indescribably angry. He had a strong urge to prove himself, even if he didn't plan to stick around here for much longer. At this point, he was certain he could skip across the Mexican border. Surely, drug trafficking was easier than... well, whatever this was.

However, for some reason he couldn't quite put his finger on, he wanted to prove to this man that he was better than nothing. And that just made him angrier.

"I said you have school!" Thomas Mast said, pulling the saw away. "And the storm's coming."

"What *is* it with you and weather?" Jacob asked. "Look at the sky! It's clear."

Thomas looked toward the sky. He nodded. "You may be right, but you still have school."

"I don't *need* school," Jacob said, making yet another move for the saw. "I want to learn how to do this."

He stopped moving. He *did* want to learn how to do this, although God only knew why. Maybe it was all that good food clouding his judgment.

Thomas Mast suddenly laughed, and like all things huge, he laughed louder than Jacob had seen any man laugh.

"On that we agree," he said between chuckles. "But the state says otherwise."

"The 'state' needs to keep its business out of ours," said Jacob.

Bizarre. He had only been there for one day, and he was already acting like he'd lived in Amish land for his whole life. But he did feel a certain kinship to this place, although why he felt that way was beyond him.

Maybe it was the contrasts; hungry in the city and well-fed here; learning new things here or getting out of jail there. The comparisons were already stacking up. And for all his warden-speak, Thomas Mast was proving to be a pretty nice guy.

Well, actually, maybe not *nice* -- he couldn't give him that after working with him for only one day. But at least he wasn't actively out to do him in.

Thomas Mast laughed yet again. "I thought I would dislike you," he said. "But I've never had an Englischer agree with me on that point. You may make it here after all."

"So -- I can stay here?" Jacob asked, suddenly far too eager to get back to work.

Thomas, the hulk of a man standing over him, seemed to ponder the question for a moment – a long moment. And then he made up his mind.

"No, I can't have that," he said. "I made a promise to make sure you were raised up right for the time being, and I intend to keep it." He raised a huge arm and pointed out beyond the woods. "Walk straight ahead down the hill to where the cart is," he said. "Walk past it and you will see a cornfield. Walk straight across, and you'll find the school."

"You aren't going to take me?" he said in surprise. Normally, back in the city, unless he was busy breaking the rules, he was accompanied by some disgruntled adult everywhere . . . not that he ever went anywhere much, except to school and back to the group home. He had been to the movies a couple of times, and to an arcade. But, being the lost dregs of the foster care system, and not being a good enough kid to be in a foster home, meant you gave up some freedoms – like a normal life. Nobody had ever trusted him enough to let him go anywhere alone.

Another comparison between *here* and *there*.

"You can walk, can't ya?" Thomas Mast gave him a steady gaze.

"I'm never allowed to go anywhere on my own," Jacob said. Again, he saw that flicker of confusion in Thomas Mast's face, quickly covered, and he rushed to explain. "In the group home, we have to be supervised all the time, so we don't even go to school on our own."

"Your legs seemed to work fine," said Mast. "Are you stupid?"

"No! I'm not stupid! Are you stupid?" Jacob tried to sound angry, but mostly he was just confused, and a little bit afraid.

This man was giving him permission to go out of his sight, and to be on his own. Being tethered to a group home with all of its restrictions and prison-like living, had been the main reason Jacob had run off so often. Now, the Amish warden was telling him to go forth on his own to school.

Is this a test? Jacob wondered. I wonder what Carol would say.

"Ne," said Mast, "I am not. If you are not stupid, and your legs work, then you can carry yourself to school. I do not need to escort you there. Do I?" Again, that steady, ice-blue stare regarded him.

"What about the storm?" Jacob was suddenly afraid.

"There is no storm," said Mast calmly. "Now git."

Jacob hesitated. He glanced down the hill, then back at Mr. Mast, who had turned back to sawing the wood.

After a few paralyzed moments, Jacob looked back down the hill again. Go to the cart, hang a right, go across a cornfield and the school is on the other side.

If I get lost, he thought, they'll never find me. This isn't like the city where there are street signs and phone booths. This is the middle of nowhere, and one cornfield looks about the same as the next.

He looked back at Mr. Mast, who had stopped sawing and was regarding him again silently. With a sigh, he put down the saw and started walking back down the hill.

Jacob stumbled and nearly fell down the hill behind him, half-running to keep up. He felt as if he had spent his day so far the same way: running behind to catch up.

At the cart, Mr. Mast stopped, waiting for him to close the distance between them.

"Climb on the buggy and look that way," Thomas Mast said, pointing across the cornfield. "Can you see the top of the school?"

"Yes, sir," Jacob replied. In the distance was a white steeple, like a shining beacon. "Thank you."

He hopped down off the buggy, realizing that his gratitude was without an audience; Mr. Mast was headed back the way he'd come.

Jacob shrugged, and started walking in the direction that had been pointed out to him.

At first, he thought about whether he could get along with

this Thomas Mast fellow, and perhaps even his family. But moments later, the thought faded from his mind completely as realization swept over him.

He was alone.

He was completely and utterly alone in a cornfield – no one around to give him instruction, or even make sure he made it to school. For the first time in his life, he was in a secluded area with not a building in sight.

Jacob looked from left to right. He wondered if he shouldn't take himself and his aching body in a direction of his choosing, and see just how far he could get. It was tempting…

But, no. In the end, he decided to walk toward the school, much though he did loathe the idea of sitting in a classroom. Give it a shot, he thought; that was his reasoning.

After all, they might be from a different century, but he thought he could like Mr. Mast after a fashion. It was better than sleeping in an alley behind a dumpster. And, they had food. That was important.

As Jacob came to the end of the cornfield, he glanced briefly at the building before him. It was still a good distance away, but he could plainly see that it was a small white building. The thought crossed his mind, and he blinked in disbelief. Was this…could it be a one-room schoolhouse?

"My God," he said. "I really have gone back in time."

As soon as the words left his mouth, it began to pour, and for the third time that day, Jacob was drenched with water.

CHAPTER THREE

As he pulled the door to the one-room schoolhouse open, he fully expected to emerge into a hallway, an airlock, or perhaps even a waiting area. Instead, he burst directly into the one-room classroom, soaked from head to toe, and cursing to boot.

He looked up slowly, realizing that every student had turned in their seat and was staring directly at him.

All his life he'd done his best not to draw attention to himself. He honestly felt that this was not helping his cause.

"Ah, I see the new student is here," the teacher said, standing up from her desk in the front. She was young, perhaps twenty years old, and wearing the same clothing as the other women he'd seen, minus the unsightly apron. Despite being young, her face was stern, and Jacob could immediately tell that, like most workers at the group home, she was a no-nonsense woman.

"Since you seem to want attention," she said, "why don't you come up here and introduce yourself?"

The rest of the class turned to stare at him once again as he made his way to the front of the room, his wet boots sloshing against the hardwood floor. It was only about thirty feet from the door to the front, but he was quickly coming to understand the concept of a few moments taking a few hours – at least in the mind.

He finally passed the front row, feeling certain that the other children were laughing at him, though he could hear nothing but his boot steps pounding against the floor. He had been in many situations in his life, he thought, but nothing like this.

He turned to face the class and prepared to introduce himself. But instead he found himself in the midst of a coughing fit, to which the rest of the class responded with cruel laughter.

"Calm it down!" The teacher's demanding voice broke through the cacophony, silencing the class. The students all stopped laughing and stared straight ahead.

Jacob inhaled once, glanced at his boots, and then prepared to speak. He found that his voice was nothing more than a squeak. Stage fright? Social anxiety? Anxiety in general? These were all terms he'd heard at the group home, when the social workers were describing their various cases. It was all very interesting, actually. In his thirteen years of existence, he'd managed to avoid having a medical label of any kind slapped onto him, besides *sociopath*. Now would be as good a time to start as any, he supposed.

"My name is Jacob," he began. His voice sounded small and quiet to him. "I came from the city...I guess I'm here because I did something wrong."

"What did you do wrong?" A young boy in the back raised his hand as he asked the question, which warranted a stern look from the teacher.

"You don't need to answer that, Jacob." She gave him a surprisingly kind smile.

"It's okay," Jacob replied. He turned and addressed the boy. "I don't know. They said I'm a sociopath, which I think means crazy, and I guess, wrong." He stared back at the teacher and saw that look of confusion on her face, which she quickly covered.

"*Are* you crazy?" the boy in the back persisted. He looked to be about Jacob's age, with blond hair, blue eyes, and that typical Pilgrim garb. When Jacob looked into his face, he only saw curiosity, not malice.

He wondered how many city kids had come through here before. Probably he was the only one they'd ever seen.

"I don't think I'm crazy," he said. "I just didn't like being locked down all the time." He smiled slightly as he said it. "I like my freedom, and in a group home, it's all about staying out of the way."

"That sounds a bit harsh," the boy replied. "We have rules, but we also have freedom."

A million thoughts started racing through Jacob's mind as he listened to the boy talking -- comparisons between the city and the country. He knew Mr. Mast had taken him in as a favor to Carol, but that didn't mean much in the grand scheme of things.

The old demons began whispering in his ear again as he stood in front of this class. He remembered the truths he took for granted, and when he heard the word *freedom*, he almost laughed out loud at the boy. He wanted to say: don't you understand what it's really like?

No one wants me.

I'm not good enough, and never will be. No one cares...

These and many other thoughts raced through his mind. But he couldn't get any of them to make the short journey from his brain to his lips.

Instead, Jacob just shrugged. He said: "I guess they didn't like the way I looked. I've learned to keep my second head hidden."

The classroom erupted into laughter, and Jacob feel a little more at ease.

The teacher, however, seemed less amused at the outburst. She directed him to an empty seat near the boy with the sandy blond hair with whom he'd just had the exchange.

"I'm Mark," the boy said, extending his hand. Jacob shook

it. And then suddenly, the exchange was over, almost as if the boy didn't wish to speak any more. Instead, he was focused on the teacher, who was opening a large black book at the front of the classroom.

"We'll start with a reading from the Book of Matthew," began the teacher, and started to read:

"Then shall the kingdom of heaven be likened unto ten virgins, which took their lamps, and went forth to meet the bridegroom. In addition, five of them were wise, and five were foolish. They that were foolish took their lamps, and took no oil with them: But the wise took oil in their vessels with their lamps.

"While the bridegroom tarried, they all slumbered and slept. And at midnight there was a cry made, Behold, the bridegroom cometh; go ye out to meet him. Then all those virgins arose, and trimmed their lamps. And the foolish said unto the wise, Give us of your oil; for our lamps are gone out. But the wise answered, saying, Not so; lest there be not enough for us and you: but go ye rather to them that sell, and buy for yourselves. And while they went to buy, the bridegroom came; and they that were ready went in with him to the marriage: and the door was shut.

"Afterward came also the other virgins, saying, Lord, Lord, open to us. But he answered and said, Verily I say unto you, I know you not. Watch therefore, for ye know neither the day nor the hour wherein the Son of man cometh."

She finished, she closed the Bible with a thud and placed it on the shelf behind her.

Jacob, for perhaps the first time in his life, was impressed. He'd been forced to attend church in the past, and had heard plenty of sermons. None of them had had any effect on him. But somehow, this was different. Everything was different here.

There was actual conviction behind the teacher's words – as if she really believed the text she was reading. That was curious, to say the least.

Without thinking, Jacob raised his hand. This prompted a strange look from the teacher.

But she said: "Yes, Jacob?"

"What did all that mean?" he asked.

There was some murmuring throughout the classroom.

"You'll have to ask your parents," she said flatly. "We don't study religion here."

"But you just read from the Bible," Jacob pushed. "Miss… uh, Mrs. … uh, ma'am."

"My name is Mrs. Zook," she said, "and it's a good way to start the day. Now, moving on to Arithmetic. Could anyone tell me..."

***

The school day dragged on for what seemed like an eternity, and Jacob felt like he had learned absolutely nothing. The subjects they covered all seemed like things he'd learned long ago, and not necessarily at school.

Now, he was sitting in the playground behind the school, full of questions – and, more importantly, with an empty stomach. However, it wasn't long before Sara Mast, the girl he (supposedly) lived with, came up to him with a brown paper bag.

"I'm supposed to give you your lunch," she said, and practically dropped it in his lap before running off to rejoin her friends.

"Well," Mark said, sitting on the stump beside Jacob, "that was interesting. Trouble at home?"

"Does *everyone* know where I live?" Jacob asked.

"Yes, actually," Mark said. "We had a meeting at the home-church just before you got here. Did you know that your favorite food is from Subway? Whatever that means. I prefer chicken myself."

"You had a meeting...about me?"

"A few week ago," Mark explained, "warning us to be alert, and for the girls to stay away from the outsider -- you. Things like that. I'm not supposed to tell you about all of this."

"That's nothing new," Jacob said. He looked off toward the

playground and opened the brown paper bag he had been handed. "I'm hated everywhere I go. Why should this place be any different?"

"'Hate' isn't the way I'd put it." Mark shrugged.

"What do you know?" Jacob said. He peered into the brown paper sack. "Peanut butter and jelly. Some things really never do change."

"We are told to stay away from you," a new girl, about Jacob's age, said as she plopped down beside him. "But I was never much for rules!"

Her voice reeked of a defiance that would probably fall apart at the first sign of confrontation, though it did make Jacob chuckle inwardly.

"Deborah, use the contractions Mrs. Weir told us about!" Mark said. "It's no wonder you're failing!"

"My mother says that I just have to know how to cook and clean," argued Deborah. "Contractions are of no use to a woman like me."

An argument suddenly broke out between the two, with Jacob stuck in the middle. He caught the first few words, but suddenly, they were speaking too quickly for him to understand, or they had switched to an entirely different language. He looked back and forth between them, but couldn't quite figure out what was going on.

The argument continued, with a fair amount of finger-pointing and screaming, until the teacher appeared on the back steps of the school and began to ring a bell, which the other children took as a sign to line up and re-enter the classroom.

The rest of the day was filled with more 'learning' -- which Jacob was learning to hate.

He thought about making a scene – something he had done at his old school, many times. But then he reconsidered. After all, if he got himself kicked out of here, next time he might find himself somewhere far worse.

Eventually, the day ended, and Jacob found himself back on the steps in front of the school, his head pounding both from the droning of the teacher and from the putrid smell of ancient textbooks.

"You all right there?" Mark asked, approaching Jacob from behind.

Jacob hesitated. "I have a question," he said.

"I was told you would have many," Mark said. He continued walking right past Jacob, forcing Jacob to walk beside him to keep up.

"Can you answer any of them?" "I can answer all but three."

"Er...which three?" Jacob asked, confused. "I cannot tell you that," Mark said.

"Helpful." Jacob snorted. "Okay. Well, what's the deal with

this place?"

"Can you be more specific?" Mark asked. They had reached the end of the property, and he leaped the roadside ditch in a single bound.

Jacob followed. "Why do you...why do you do these things?" he asked. "Why don't you have electricity? Why do you dress like this?"

"We get along fine without your electricity," Mark pointed out. "And, last I checked, you dress like this, too."

"You're funny."

"Fact of the matter," said Mark, as he led the way across another yard, "is that I know where you came from. And, against my parents' judgment, I don't want you to go back there."

"Sorry, but I want to go back there," Jacob said assertively. He wasn't quite sure of its truth as he said it, but it seemed true enough for the moment. "This...whatever this is –"he gestured around them -- "it's just a step along the way. I mean, seriously, this is like...a Norman Rockwell painting."

"Who is this Normal Rockwell?"

"Normal," Jacob tried to correct him. "Dammit! Norman!"

"You might tone the language down a bit," Mark said. He had turned red, as if he'd never heard a curse word before in his life. "Mr. Mast will punish you if he hears you, even if you are an Englischer boy."

Jacob could see they were approaching yet another white building: one which reminded him of the one room schoolhouse they had just left.

He told Mark: "He said that if I stayed, I would be a part of his family, and subject to all his rules and consequences."

"That would be true. We Amish..." Mark stopped. "We believe in God and family very deeply. You can't live with a family and not be included."

Jacob looked at the building in front of them. "What is this place?"

"It's our central meeting place," said Mark. He walked up a set of concrete steps and pulled open the door.

"Why did I follow you up here?" Jacob wondered aloud, as he followed Mark into the building.

Unlike the school, this building actually seemed to have multiple rooms. The first they came into was a long coatroom, or, at least, that was what it looked like. He almost asked for an explanation, but instead opted to follow Mark in silence through a series of hallways, until they came to an open room somewhere in the right wing of the building. It was a simple-looking, plain room, attached to what Jacob took to be a kitchen. In the main area was a long, long table.

"This is what it's all about," Mark said quietly.

"This table?"

"No," Mark said, suddenly not seeming in the mood for humor. "Our way of life here in Hope Crossing. It's all about our submission to God. If you trust Him, He will show you the way. That's the way I've always found it."

"And you actually believe that?" Jacob asked, incredulously. "Look, what you have here is nice, but it's all just a fantasy."

"If it is, it's a fantasy that's stood for hundreds of years," said Mark. "And it's one you could stand to learn from."

Jacob found himself getting a bit angry. "Look," he said. "I wasn't wanted in the city. I won't be wanted here. That's just the way it goes for me."

"Joseph wasn't wanted," Mark pointed out. He took a seat at the long table, apparently not bothered that no one else was there.

"Who? Who's Joseph?" Jacob asked.

"Joseph was a boy from Bible times--"

"Look," Jacob said, interrupting Mark's speech. "I've been to church, I never bought it. It's just a bunch of rules that tell us what we can and can't do. We can't laugh, can't smile, can't have fun--"

"I don't know what those English churches are teachin' you," Mark said, his voice full of energy, "but I've never run into a verse that says we can't have fun." He shook his head. "That's what happens when they start discussin' the good book in the house of the Lord. Everyone starts formin' their own opinion, and practically writes a new book while they're at it…"

"So, people shouldn't have opinions?"

"I'm not an expert," Mark said. "Not by a far sight. But – look, when you read a book, do you take it to mean anything but what it says?"

"Not really. But then," Jacob admitted, "I haven't read that many books."

Mark said, "When you read the Bible, it says one thing, and you should do that one thing. When Moses walked down the mountain with the Ten Commandments, they didn't read: 'Thou shalt not kill, *unless*…' You see what I'm saying? There's no discussion there."

"Okay," said Jacob, "but what if someone's going to kill you? Like, what if they come at you with a knife?"

"Then you die and get your reward in heaven. It's all about turning the other cheek."

Jacob stared at him. "That's insane."

"Joseph turned the other cheek," Mark said. "Let's talk about Joseph some more."

Jacob shrugged and shook his head. "Fine, we'll talk about Joseph, then. Who was Joseph?"

"Joseph was a boy in the Bible, maybe about our age. He wasn't wanted, either, though not entirely of his own doing."

"Like me."

Mark gave him a friendly glance, but didn't comment. He went on: "He told his brothers that one day, they would bow before him. And then his father awarded him a coat of many colors, and that made his brothers jealous."

Jacob listened, pulling out a chair and sitting down at the table. Mark went on: "So, they threw him in a pit one day, while they were tending to the fields." Jacob shook his head, but it didn't surprise him; that was how the world worked. "His kinder brother, Reuben, had always intended to rescue him, but his more jealous brothers decided to sell him to slavers, who took him far away.

"Once there, he had a hard time of it, for sure. But then he rose to a position of power. And then finally, during a famine, his brothers came to him, begging for grain rations. You see, he was unwanted. But in the end, it was up to him to decide their fate. Isn't that neat?"

Jacob waited for Mark to continue the story, but he didn't seem inclined to go on. "Well, what happened?" Jacob asked, to prod him.

"The end isn't really important," Mark said. "What matters is that Joseph was unwanted and sent away, but then he became a better man for it." He tilted his head and looked at Jacob.

"Maybe you, too, can become a better man because of it."

Jacob frowned. "Life isn't a fairy tale or a Bible story," he said, feeling the bitterness rising in him. "Things don't happen that way. Not now, not ever."

Unwanted, and a better man for it… yeah, right. Instead of a better man, he would probably wind up in juvie, or adult jail, or worse. It wasn't his destiny to be anything but a foster kid until he became a street adult. At best, he could hope to go into the military; join the Marines, and get killed in some war in the Middle East -- that is, if he was lucky.

"I want to be a Marine," he confided to Mark.

"What's a Marine?"

It was Jacob's turn to be incredulous.

"You know… be all that you can be, serve in the United States

Marine Corps? Fight in a war, and, hopefully, die a heroic death."

That was about all Jacob knew about the Marines himself. But he did have a pamphlet that a Marine recruiter had given him a couple years of back, on one of his unscheduled outings. It showed pictures of honorable-looking men and women standing proudly in their uniforms. They were hard-edged, neatly dressed and terrifying, with big muscles and fierce spirits. According to the pamphlet, they fought for the United

States, and went on to be 'The Few – The Proud - The Marines.'

"We don't fight in wars." Mark stopped Jacob in his tracks.

"What?"

"We don't believe in violence," said Mark.

"Well, that's a downer." Jacob didn't know what else to say. "I want to be part of something like the Corps. When you get through boot camp, they give you a bunk, a uniform and a rank. You become somebody in the Corps."

"You are somebody now, aren't you?" said Mark.

"Well, yes. But you become somebody people will look at and not laugh at. And the recruiter was telling me it's perfect for foster kids with no homes. The military gives you a home, food and money."

"Don't you have a home here with food? And probably money, too, if you do a good job." Mark's expression was quizzical. Clearly, Mark didn't understand the importance of the Marines.

"Well, yes, but he only took me in because he owes my social worker a favor. I don't think he wants me."

"You may be mistaken about Mr. Mast," said Mark. "He stood up in the group and said that he was taking you in whether the community felt unified or not. For us, that is a huge risk. He said that you had no home, and that he was blessed with a daughter but no son. He wanted to give you a chance, because from what he had read of your case file, no one had ever given you a break."

"He said that?" The tree with hair and hat had stood up for him? Jacob was flabbergasted at the possibility.

"Yes. That social worker of yours really talked up your case, I understand. We were told to be careful of you, though -- not because you are horrible, but because you don't know our ways."

"Oh, wow!"

This could put another slant on things entirely.

But, then again, it could be a way of setting him up for a really big fall. Just when he sat back and got comfortable, they would let the other shoe drop...

"Things happen the way God wants them to," Mark said, smiling. For the moment, Jacob could almost let that doofy optimism slide by. "And, right now, it's time for me to get home."

CHAPTER FOUR

From the bag he'd packed at the shelter, Jacob pulled the one thing that still managed to remind him of home – a pack of brand-name cigarettes.

He'd obtained them back in the city in the usual way, by bribing a homeless man with change from a $10 bill. Nearly half the pack had been smoked now, and he'd stuffed a lighter stuffed in the empty space that was left.

What he hadn't known when he'd smoked them was that they might very well be the last cigarettes he ever managed to get his hands on – at least, until he entered adulthood, or ran away from this place. Which, he told himself, he still fully intended to do, as soon as he could get around to working out a plan.

The most important lesson he'd managed to learn over all his years so far was that people were out for themselves, and only themselves. No one wanted to lend a helping hand unless it benefited them somehow. And when setting out on his own, he would have to take that into account.

Money would be necessary, especially when trying to get from here to there. Clean clothes were also a must. He'd learned that walking around in tattered or dirty clothing was a dead giveaway to any police officer who either cared, or simply felt like filling a quota.

There were a million other things that would need to be covered – things that the average runaway never really considered. For example, if he was caught, he could expect to spend up to a year in jail. A person wouldn't have assumed that the police were great at capturing runaways, with all the other things going on in the city, but Jacob had become convinced that the city police had become committed to finding and dragging runaways to the city jail by their ears.

Cops were freaky like that. Since, apparently, kids are now quickly becoming murderers – America has an epidemic of child killers, according to the news – there'd been an increase in child arrests. The cops wanted to protect and serve (the rich and powerful), and that meant that all the punk kids like him needed to be locked up.

After all, if you're locked up, you can't commit mayhem against the unsuspecting rich people zipping around the city in their high-priced cars, with their high-priced wives and their favored children, whose single outfit of clothing was more than what was allotted to his kind for a year.

He had left the house, still holding the pack of cigarettes, and was walking through the trees, where he assumed (but wasn't sure) that no one else ever walked. If he had been a bit older and perhaps a bit wiser, he might have been able to appreciate the majesty of the forest before him, and how far removed it was from the rest of humanity.

Instead, he was more focused on the smokes in his pocket – the last he might have in a long, long time.

Then again, he suddenly thought, wouldn't it be better to just cut the addiction now?

He reflected for a moment, trying to decide whether he should take those last few puffs.

It wasn't a hard decision, actually. For him, smoking had been more of a recreational thing than an addiction. And right now, he was feeling an urge to find out how the story of Joseph ended – something that he most certainly was not going to discover hanging around smoking in the woods.

He searched around, found a tree whose roots were largely above ground, and dug a small hole in the earth with his hands. It wasn't very deep, but then again, it didn't have to be. He deposited the pack of cigarettes there, covered it with earth and leaves, and walked away. Even as he walked back to the house, he was trying to decide whether he was rationing them or simply leaving them behind.

On the way back, the sky began yet again to fill with gray clouds. A less-than-subtle hint of rain permeated the air. He didn't speed up his steps, though. What did it matter if he got a little bit wet . . . again?

***

The moment he stepped through the back door into the Mast family house, all he could think was, "Oh, crap."

After leaving the cigarettes, he had walked a long, circuitous route around the outer edge of a field. It took him at least 45 minutes, by his figuring, to reach the house. He had been caught up in the freedom, the smell of the air, the breeze in his hair and the quiet.

When he stepped into the kitchen, all that Zen peace he had felt was replaced by wariness and fear. Yes, fear – for real.

They were all waiting there in the kitchen, sitting at the long wooden table, and staring at him as if he'd done something horribly wrong.

Jacob felt his heart sink, as his adrenaline rose. Was all that stuff Mark had shared with him a lie? Were they waiting to get rid of him after all?

"Where were you?" Thomas asked quietly. The man didn't even have to rise from the table to sound intimidating. It gave Jacob pause for a moment.

"I was out with someone I met at the school," he answered, more or less truthfully. After all, he had been out with Mar. The whole thing with the cigarettes didn't need mentioning.

"He's lying!" Sara shouted, her high-pitched voice reverberating around the kitchen. She was small, stocky and short, and right now he thought she looked like a deranged gnome without the red hat. She was three years his junior, and the Mast's only child, as far as he knew; but she seemed able to fill up the house all by herself.

"I saw what he did!" she insisted.

"I'm not lying!" Jacob practically spat out at her. It was an automatic reaction, born of years of being in the foster care system. Never admit to anything, ever.

"I went over to the central meeting place with Mark!" he said. "He showed me around after school, and we got to talking. I lost track of time, and I'm sorry. I didn't know that I would get the same crap I get at the group home."

He heard Sara and Dorothy gasp. Now what had he done? He stared at the two of them, confused.

"He's lying," Sara whispered. "I saw him when he came home, and that was over an hour ago."

"Who are you, anyway, you little bitc --"

"Enough."

Thomas Mast stood up and slammed his hand down on the table. He moved so suddenly that Jacob stumbled back, away from where he had been standing before the table. "We do not use that kind of language in this family. And you will respect the women and girls in this family, or you will pay the price for your transgression."

Oh no. Jacob found himself gulping. He was still backing slowly away from the monster-man who towered above him.

It was clear he was about to die, pounded to death by a tree in a straw hat with steam coming out of his ears, fire shooting from his mouth and a voice that silenced giants. What was that story he'd read once? Goliath? He was an ant by comparison.

"Mark who?" Dorothy Mast interjected suddenly.

Jacob thought of her as a larger version of her gnome daughter, with blonde hair pulled back into a bun with a neatly clipped hat on top, farmer-woman clothing, and an apron. Under other circumstances, she might have appeared to be kindly. But he didn't think her kind at this moment: just another accuser and enemy.

However, right now she was a welcome distraction. He circled around, outside the range of the tree-monster, and moved around the table toward her.

"I..." Jacob tried desperately to recall his new friend's last name, keeping his eyes on Thomas-tree-monster all the while. But he quickly realized, to his despair, that he'd never asked and never been told. He hadn't imagined he would be needing the information to deal with an interrogation later.

"See? He's a liar!" Sara said smugly, crossing her arms. Dorothy held up her hand to quiet her. "But he's lying!" Sara insisted. "And --"

"I do not know who you befriended," said Thomas. "It might be good that you get to know other Amish children and learn more of our ways, if you're going to stay here. That is not the issue." He, too, raised a hand to shush his daughter, and Sara finally fell silent. "I can tell you what I do care about, though, and that is you're lying, cursing and smoking at your age on my property." He produced the pack of cigarettes that Jacob had buried no more than an hour and a half before.

Jacob's stomach dropped, nearly to his feet. How had they even found it? How could they possibly have been watching him? Sara -- that mouthy little dwarf -- must have followed him. And as he'd wended his way back, breathing in the clean air and thinking about freedom, she had dug up his secret and beaten a hasty trail back to her parents.

"I must not have made it clear when you arrived," Thomas said, carefully laying the pack of cigarettes on the table. "There are to be no shenanigans. And you are not to break the rules of this house. Now, maybe I didn't fully explain those rules. I thought them to be common sense. But I will explain this now: There is to be no smoking in or around my house, period. While you are here, you will abide by the Amish way of life, whether you plan to stick with it or not. Though, from what I've seen so far, I think I'd rather you didn't."

There was a brief silence, and in that silence, Jacob could have said any number of things. He could have denied that he'd been smoking, or he could have apologized.

Unfortunately, Thomas was a man unlike any he'd seen at the group home, or even on the tyrannical police force. In all Jacob's encounters with adults to date, he had been able to keep his cool, and remain in control of the situation -- or at least so he thought. In this case, however, he was losing his footing.

He had to find some way to get it back. "What's wrong with smoking, anyway?" he whispered.

Even as he spoke, he berated himself. Why had he even for a moment expected this to go any differently? Why was he even trying?

"Other than the fact that our body is a temple -- which you wouldn't understand, anyhow --" Thomas was making a beeline for Jacob. Jacob felt as if he were about to be overtaken by a freight train.

Thomas bent down, placing his head at Jacob's eye level. "You are too young to smoke."

He went on: "Let me tell you what. There is not going to be smoking; there will not be time for smoking.

"Now, you are here, as I told you, because I owe Carol a favor. But you are not going to interrupt my life, or my family's life.

"From here on out, you are going to come straight home from school, you're going to do your chores, and on Sunday you're going to go to church. There won't be no heathen living in my household."

"What if I told you that there never *was* a heathen living in your household?" Jacob said smartly. He regretted the words even as they tumbled out of his mouth. He knew that he had a death wish -- and now he knew how he was going to die, pounded to death by an Amish tree.

"Oh, that's funny. That is real funny. I tell you what, boy," Thomas said, placing a massive finger against the bridge of Jacob's nose. He looked to Jacob as if he was nearly foaming at the mouth. "None of this -- and I mean, *none* of this -- leaves this house. I don't want rumors of hooliganism, or whatever it is you brought with you, getting out into our community. My family has a reputation to uphold. *And,* if you're going to be part of this family, then that means you have a reputation, too."

"Why should I care about your reputation?" Jacob demanded, pushing Thomas's finger away. "I didn't ask to come here. *And,* I don't have a family; I've never had a family. I just live in places until they can't stand me or use me anymore." Jacob felt moisture on his face, and quickly brushed it aside. "This place is no different, and you people are no different." He felt suddenly tired, defeated. "Oh, what difference does it make, anyway?"

The giant man stood there regarding him silently. "You were given a choice, or so I hear," Thomas said quietly. "You could either go to one of those Englischer jails, or you could come here. You chose to come here. Now you are here. So, if you are going to be here, then *be* here."

"I *am* here. More than you care to know." Jacob shrugged and looked away. "I came today to ask questions. But just like everyone else, you treat me like I'm stupid – dirt on your shoe -- just because I'm young, and not Amish like your daughter -- or like the rest of the people who had to have a meeting to figure out how to treat me like trash."

"Pay mind to how you speak of my daughter," Thomas said angrily. "She lives here, just like you."

"Then how about this?" Jacob said. "I'm gone."

"That's real funny," Thomas said, turning and walking toward the opposite end of the kitchen.

"Do I look like I'm laughing?" Jacob turned toward the door. "I think I'd rather be in jail. At least I *know* there that they don't give a shit about me."

He felt a hand come down on him, grabbing him by the collar. Before he could say another word, he was being hustled out the door, and heard the wooden door slamming shut behind him.

What the hell? Where was this man taking him? Maybe he was going to kill him…

But he heard Mast talking as they walked. Well, anyway, Mast was walking. For Jacob, it was more like being dragged toward the barn.

"It's a four-hour drive from here to the city. You don't have a car, and we don't have a phone. Even if you find a phone, do you have the number?

"I'm sure not wasting my time," Mast went on. "We don't curse in this family. If you insist on disobeying my rules, you will pay the consequences. Just like Sara."

Mast dragged him unceremoniously into the barn. "Boy, you *will* learn to respect our family and our ways."

He sat down on a hay bale, pulling Jacob across his lap and positioning him face down. Then he started to smack Jacob's bottom.

Jacob struggled frantically to get loose. Was this man kidding? He was *thirteen* -- street smart, wiseass, and tough as they come. But the smacks continued, and, in spite of his best efforts, Jacob began to cry.

He wasn't a baby. He didn't want to let this man see him break down. But his rear end was on fire by now, and he couldn't help the sobs. It didn't slow the steady stream of smacks he received. This felt even worse than getting beat up in a street fight.

Eventually, it ended. Thomas stood, and put Jacob, shakily, on his feet.

"You will respect our ways and our family," he repeated

again. "Or you will reap the consequences." He looked at him, blue eyes fixed and steady. "I do not like spankings. But if you can't behave, you will receive them. We, as Amish parents, know that sometimes it needs to be done in order to make naughty children nice."

Jacob had nothing to say to that. Instead, he stared straight ahead.

Once more, he was contemplating walking back to the city. But that would do him no good at this point, as Thomas had been kind enough to point out.

"You will scrape the stalls clean before I bring in the livestock," he heard Thomas say. "I'll be out there shortly."

Thomas stood up, waiting for Jacob to respond. Jacob continued to sniffle softly, avoiding looking at him.

"Is that clear, boy?"

"Yes, sir." Jacob responded finally.

If this was what life was to be like for any length of time, then was staying here really, truly worth it? He weighed these questions as he crossed the threshold into the barn stalls, which had been left open earlier in the day.

"When we are done, we will go in and have our supper." Mast seemed to be finished with this phase of their relationship. Without another word, he turned and went out of the barn.

Well, at least he hadn't spanked and embarrassed him completely in front of Sara and her mother. That would have been unlivable; Sara would never let him live that one down.

What the hell do I do here? he wondered. But he found his question quickly answered when his eyes came to rest on a large shovel. It reminded Jacob, more than anything else, of the snow shovels that were used in the city, particularly those he and his 'friends' had been forced to use to clear the group home's parking lot. Presumably, on that day, the administrator had decided it would do them good to put in some physical labor. Then again, it was probably well-deserved. They had, after all, relocated his car.

Jacob took the shovel from the wall and walked around the corner, moving deeper into the barn. The stalls stood open, each one of them, and the moment he crossed the second threshold, an incredibly putrid smell hit his nostrils. He gagged, shocked. This had to be the worst thing he'd ever smelled, and he had grown up in the city, so that was quite a statement!

He shuddered, and moved to the first stall, ready and willing to take on the challenge.

Like the others, it was open, but also dark, so he couldn't see what was causing the aforementioned awful smell.

As he moved forward, there was a click and a buzz. A bank of fluorescent lights activated, flooding the entire barn with cool, white light. Seconds later, Thomas came around the corner, pushing a massive yellow wheelbarrow, which he left next to Jacob without a word.

Of course. Of *course*, he was supposed to put the... crap... in the wheelbarrow.

It took him the better part of an hour to clean the first stall... or, at least, so it seemed to Jacob. By the time he was done, his back was aching, his arms felt as though they were on fire, and his rear end was tender and throbbed whenever he took a step. Could it be actually be possible that Thomas did this regularly?

He staggered out, exhausted and short of breath. But still, he'd done it! He'd actually cleaned the stall!

His victory, however, was rather short-lived. Blinking in the white light, he realized that Thomas had been busy as well/ All but one of the remaining stalls were clean.

Had Thomas decided that time was of the essence? Or was he just trying to show Jacob that he could never be good enough to live this lifestyle?

It didn't matter, Jacob decided. It was obvious that he wasn't going to be here long enough, anyway.

He was still shaking his head when he heard Thomas's voice boom from another stall: "Take it out back."

'Out back'? Jacob puzzled for a moment. He could only assume Thomas meant for him to go through the doors at the opposite end of the barn.

With that in mind, he grasped the two wooden handles of the wheelbarrow and tried lifting them. This was actually quite easy. Then, he pushed the wheelbarrow forward… only to find that it wouldn't budge.

"What?" he said aloud. He let go of the handles, letting the wheelbarrow drop flat, and walked to the front to investigate.

The problem was obvious. "The tire is flat," he said loudly.

"We don't use air in our tires," came Thomas's voice from— it seemed – yet another stall (Jacob could have sworn he was somewhere else a minute ago). "You're relying on modern conveniences again."

"You have electric lights in here!" Jacob yelled. Then he stopped himself. After all, he didn't want to get spanked twice in one night.

Maybe, he thought, he should just shut up and stay quiet until he could get emancipated. It all seemed very strange: after all, he'd always wanted a family. But now that he was being *forced* to be part of a family, it didn't fit his fantasy at all.

"I don't consider fire safety a modern 'convenience.'" Apparently, Thomas had decided to overlook the defiance – and loudness – of Jacob's last comment.

Jacob grumbled, but only under his breath, and headed back around to grab the wheelbarrow's handles again. He lifted once more; then he pushed with all his might. His feet dug into the earth floor of the barn, but the wheelbarrow didn't move. He pushed harder. His boots weren't helping any; they had lost traction long ago, worn down by their previous wearer.

Finally, the wheelbarrow started to inch forward, very, very slowly, toward the barn exit. The further he pushed it, the easier it became.

He suddenly had a flashback to a physics lesson he'd had back home. Something about an object in motion tending to stay in motion.

Well, that seemed to be true right now. The wheelbarrow was really rolling now; it showed no signs of stopping.

That was when Jacob realized he probably couldn't stop it even if he wanted to.

This seemed like it might be a serious problem.

He tightened his grip on the wooden handles, as the massive cart raced toward the manure heap, a huge pile of feces and straw, that been built up behind the barn.

"Whoa, stop!" he yelled to the wheelbarrow, as if it would hear and heed his command. "Stop, stop stop stop!"

But the wheelbarrow obeyed no command but its own. It crashed into a rock, wheel-first. The impact immediately threw Jacob off the handles, and into...

... the pile of manure before him. He landed squarely in it, with a pathetic squishing sound. The wheelbarrow landed squarely on top of him, dumping its load of feces in a second pile neatly over his head.

Jacob lay there, unmoving. He had never felt more pathetic in his life.

I am -- he thought -- literally in a deep pile of manure.

Thomas's distinct voice boomed from the barn.

"Come here so I can clean you off," he said. "You'll need to take off those clothes; you smell like a horse."

If Jacob wasn't mistaken, he thought he heard amusement in the Mast-tree's tone.

Glad I can be so funny to you, he thought.

This day just kept getting better and better.

CHAPTER FIVE

"I'm finding a phone," Jacob announced as he, Dorothy, and Sara dismounted the carriage.

They had come into the town proper, supposedly on some sort of shopping trip. Jacob wondered why they couldn't simply grow whatever they needed, since that seemed to be the thing around these parts. But Dorothy Mast had said something about needing flour.

He had been stuck with the Masts for over two weeks now. He wasn't sure exactly how long; he was starting to lose track of the days. And he was also starting to get scared: he was coming to like these people. He was beginning to like this place, and to think of them as family.

The part of him that was a hard-knock city boy shouted at him that he should get going, get himself out of here, before he became too attached to them, and they changed him permanently.

No one stopped him as he wandered off in search of a pay phone, although, after a good thirty minutes of searching, he came to realize that a pay phone was going to be extremely difficult to find.

He had wandered past the grocery store several times, glancing at the giant banner that screamed: "Yes! We have Whoopie Pies!" -- what the heck was a Whoopie Pie? – before it occurred to him that, if there was one anywhere, there might be a phone in the grocery store.

He turned around and entered, pushing his way through the glass doors.

"Hello!" said the woman at the counter. "Welcome. Can I help you with anything?" She was younger than Dorothy, though, Jacob guessed, not by much.

Jacob stopped a fair distance away; he was still wary enough not to get too close. "I'm trying to find a phone," he said.

"Oh, I know who you are!" the woman said, with a warm grin.

"You're the boy from the city – Jacob, is it?" Jacob took a step forward, confused. After all, they were in town here.

"You know me?" he asked, feeling a bit of color rushing to his cheeks. Did the whole world know he was living with the Masts?

"Everyone knows you, silly!" said a familiar voice, as

Deborah Waver appeared from behind a row of shelves near the back of the store. "Did not you know that?"

"Contractions, Deborah," the shopkeeper said. "You must learn to use contractions."

"Why 'must' I learn to use contractions?" Deborah asked smugly. "You understood me, right?"

"Because *I* like to use them," the shopkeeper said, "and when you don't use them, it makes me feel awkward in the conversation."

"Is that not your problem instead of mine?" Deborah grinned wider.

"Deborah, dear," said the woman. "There's a box of jelly in the back. Be a dear and stock it, would you?"

"Fine," said Deborah cheerfully, "I will stock it." She turned and skipped off.

Though the encounter had been extremely brief, Jacob had had a chance to get a good look at Deborah.

Though she was dressed in those hideously plain clothes, he couldn't help but find her attractive. His feelings were not unlike those he'd had for his friend Sherry long ago. But from what he'd seen of this place, he couldn't imagine a girl here being interested in that sort of thing. Still...wouldn't it be nice?

The shopkeeper broke into his reverie. "Why don't you take some ice cream, dear?"

Jacob shrugged. "I don't have any money."

"That's OK. Today, your money's no good here."

"I don't understand..." Jacob suddenly struggled to make eye contact. "Why would you do that for me?"

"You're here, aren't you?" she asked. Her voice lowered. "Instead of in jail... That's a nice thing someone's done for you. Really, where would we be if people didn't do nice things for one another?"

Jacob had a brief flashback to the city he'd come from. He remembered the rundown streets, the tattered buildings, and the gangs infesting every corner, waiting for the right person to make the wrong turn. Then, of course, there were the authority figures, who were no better than the criminals on most days...

That, in his mind, was a great example, of "where we'd be if people didn't do nice things for one another."

But, on the other hand, it was the only life he had ever known. And he still found himself struggling to understand why anyone would offer a helping hand, if it didn't benefit them.

"What do *you* get out of it?" he asked, moving slightly closer to her.

"I get a nice warm feeling. That's what I get." She smiled, as she emerged from behind the counter and bent over a small freezer located to the left of the cash register. "Now, what do you like? Chocolate or vanilla?"

"Chocolate..." he muttered, as she reached into the freezer and pulled out a small cardboard cup.

He still didn't trust her -- not as far as he could have thrown her, and that certainly wasn't far.

"The best part about these cups," she said, as she turned and came over to hand it to him, "is that they come with their own spoon stuck to the bottom. I never could get over how cool that is!"

And with that, Jacob found himself outside once again, heading back toward where the Mast buggy had been parked.

He realized he had completely forgotten to ask her what a Whoopie Pie was. After a brief debate, he decided against going back and pressing his luck. She had been nice to him once, but that might change, with continued exposure to him. Best leave sleeping dogs -- and demons -- lie.

Dorothy Mast leaned out as he approached the black buggy. "I thought you were going to find a phone?" she said.

"Out of order," he lied.

After a moment's thought, he handed over the cup of ice cream to Sara. "I got this for you," he said. Maybe, just maybe, he's be able to pass along that warm, fuzzy feeling the storekeeper had been talking about.

Sara was starting to grow on him. She was looking less like an ugly gnome, and more like a smaller version of Dorothy. Dorothy was a great cook, patient, and, he thought, kind. She let him taste stuff she was making; she'd taken to wordlessly offering him a spoonful of something when he came home. It always tasted good. On occasion, she even smiled back at him when he said thank you – *denki* – the Amish way.

Sara reached out, suspiciously, and took the ice cream.

"Did you steal it?" she asked. Her inflection made it sound more like a statement than a question.

"Nope," Jacob said, nowhere near as offended by the question as he should have been.

"But you have no money!" Dorothy Mast pressed. "We don't steal."

"I know," Jacob said. "I didn't. I guess you don't need money for everything." He shrugged, but it still bothered him.

So they thought he'd stolen it. Was his reputation so bad, he wondered, that they automatically thought of him as a thief?

Nah, another voice in him said. They're just worried about the family reputation. And they didn't realize yet that he wouldn't have dared to steal it and risk another spanking from Thomas.

It seemed as if the conversation was going to go further. But they were interrupted by the sound of laughter.

Jacob turned toward the sound. Two boys, both at least five years his senior, were standing on the corner, snapping pictures of the buggy, and, of course, of Sara and Dorothy.

Jacob immediately approached them.

"What the hell are you doing?" he whispered, low enough that the women would not be able to make out his words.

"We're taking in the scenery," said one of the boys. "What else?" "We're not scenery; we're people."

"Kinda look like time travelers to me," the other boy said. "What are you going to do about it, Pilgrim?"

The weird thing, of course, was that a few weeks earlier, he would have been the one standing there laughing at the Pilgrims. But he'd been learning that these Pilgrims were people, and really nice.

Jacob wanted to hit these boys and shut them up. They had no idea what they were talking about, and it was not ---

He heard Thomas speaking in his head. It is not our way to do violence in the face of ignorance. Turn the other cheek.

"Jacob, come back here," Dorothy called. "We need to get home now."

There was that rage building up inside him again, as was to be expected...

But, for some reason, he did not act on it.

Instead, he bit his lower lip, turned away from the boys, and began to walk back toward the buggy.

He heard their laughter behind him, and recited the words to himself like a litany: *Turn the other cheek . . . turn the other cheek....turn the other cheek.*

"That's right!" one of the boys shouted. "Listen to Mommy and go back to your time machine!"

He started to turn around again, but felt a firm hand gripping his shoulder. It was Dorothy. For once, she almost appeared to have a visibly sympathetic look on her face... but he couldn't really be sure.

Just let it go, he decided. What was the phrase? "Let go; let God." It might not be exactly the way the Amish would say it, but the meaning was the same.

"We deal with it all the time," Dorothy said. Her voice seemed gentle to him. "But they answer to God, not us."

"Okay," he replied softly. "I won't rip their heads off -- well, this time -- and ruin the family name."

Dorothy smiled. She pointed at the groceries she had bought. Jacob loaded them into the back of the buggy, and climbed in himself after them.

The ride home was tedious for Jacob, as he sat in the back of the buggy, separated by a massive bag of flour from Sara, who was clearly enjoying her ice cream.

On one hand, he was glad he had done what he knew was considered the 'right' thing. But had it really been right?

He had called this a fantasy world once, and he'd really meant it. How could these people possibly manage to stay alive in a world where they renounced violence, even in the name of self-defense? That seemed even stranger than renouncing electricity – the other thing he'd never quite managed to wrap his head around.

Then again, there was one good thing about being here. For the first time in his life, he was -- sort of, almost -- experiencing what it might be like to have a family. It had never been all that high on his bucket list, because he'd always had his fantasy family to fall back on. But it was... nice... to have the opportunity.

That night, he did the chores he'd been assigned without complaint, and even managed to clean the stalls without burying himself alive in fecal matter (he hadn't learned yet that cleaning the stalls again so soon after the last time was utterly unnecessary, and he'd accomplished nothing more than waste a few bales of hay).

Just before going into the house for dinner, he paused to take notice of a tree in the front yard. It looked like any other tree, and he'd passed it before without noticing, but there was something... important... about it.

Though he knew the call for dinner would come any time, he got more and more curious, until he found himself standing no more than a few feet from it.

It was an apple tree. A real apple tree.

Apples were eaten daily at the group home. And, in school, he'd learned that they came from trees. But for some reason, those had always seemed more fairy tales than anything else.

Stories of a man named Johnny traveling across America, planting seeds and wearing a pot on his head had always seemed a stretch too far for him. Could it really be possible for someone to...

He stopped in mid-thought, and looked around. Yes. Yes, it was.

"God's gifts are all around is," Thomas Mast said, from the front porch. "All you have to do is look."

Jacob wasn't entirely surprised to see him, though he hadn't noticed him come out.

"Where I come from," he said wryly, "God's gifts are covered in pesticide and sitting on a grocery-store shelf."

"But first, they come from a tree like this one," Thomas said. "When you see something like this -- even a little thing like this – it gets awful hard to deny God, does it not?" He shook his head mildly. "Englischers... no offense... try to tell us the universe came from an explosion, like gunpowder, and that all of this is by chance. But how could any of *this* be by chance?" His gesture took in the hills, the sky, and the whole world around them.

Jacob shrugged. He was still not entirely inclined to believe, but he was also not inclined to argue.

He went on wondering how these people managed to continue living this way and believing in fairy tales. But it wasn't his place to offer any other explanation, either. As much as he found he wanted to believe Thomas – and, to his own surprise, he really did want to -- he had his experiences, and he knew what he'd learned from them.

On the other hand, Thomas was clearly a real person, too. For instance, he clearly loved his wife; Jacob had seen them in the kitchen kissing and gazing at each other in that way that led to other acts of affection. He'd stopped himself, standing just out of sight, and then quietly withdrawn to allow them their privacy. Why he'd done that, he didn't know. It had just seemed like the right thing to do.

As time passed, he found himself, it seemed, more and more inclined to do the right thing.

"I heard you turned the other cheek today." Thomas was speaking again. "You didn't have to, but you did. I owe you a debt of gratitude for that."

"You do?" said Jacob, deeply startled. Thomas never stopped surprising him. For instance, like yesterday, when he had started showing Jacob how to make a chair. You would think that would be the most boring activity on the planet – at least, Jacob would have thought so -- but Thomas explained things patiently, quietly, and with care, and let him help. It turned out to be one of the most interesting projects he had ever worked on.

"You made my house look good," Thomas said. "There are people watching, believe it or not. There are always people watching. It won't be forgotten."

Jacob shrugged again. Facing the boys on the pavement, turning away at Dorothy's call – to tell the truth, he hadn't considered it 'turning the other cheek,' in the sense of iron-willed self-control. Rather, he was simply doing what he was told instead of further pressing his luck. In his mind, there was a huge difference, even if Thomas couldn't quite see it.

He suddenly realized that Thomas could no more guess what was going on in his mind, than he could guess what was really going on in Thomas'. Adults weren't really as all-knowing as they pretended to be, were they?

"Why don't you come in and have your supper?" Thomas said, heading toward the door. "Can't let all that flour go to waste."

"We're eating flour?" said Jacob, hurrying after him.

If he wasn't mistaken, Thomas was smiling. That was usually reserved for Dorothy and Sara, not him.

So much had changed in the past few weeks.

CHAPTER SIX

Attending home-church with the Mast family was nice. Every two weeks, as they'd explained, they went to a different family's home.

It already seemed like an eternity since he'd left the group home, taking the long drive from the city to the small village of Hope Crossing. Now he sat in the Stoltzfus' house, listening to Bishop Zook read the lesson. He didn't always listen to the Bishop; often his mind wandered off, reflecting silently on the recent weeks.

He tried to concentrate on the sermon. The first time he'd gone, no one had mentioned the entire thing would be presented in another language, making it impossible for him to get much out of it. In spite of that, he listened, and from time to time glanced around the homes they visited.

He'd been to church before, but this was a little different. For some reason, the men and women sat on opposite sides of the room. And the walls were bare enough that each word the

Bishop spoke echoed and boomed through the building as if it were the word of God himself.

Though they seemed to take forever and a day, the sermons eventually ended. But, unlike at most church services he had been to, no one seemed in a hurry to leave once the service was concluded. Instead, people congregated in the coatroom up front, and there were many standing on the front lawn.

It had been a little confusing at first. But Jacob had quickly realized that, in a world where chores and work were a weeklong affair, it only made sense that everyone would want to spend time together and catch up on Sundays. After all, they didn't have Facebook, did they?

The only problem was that Jacob felt more than a little left out of this equation.

"Jacob," a voice shouted, "Jacob, over here!"

It was Mark. At school, right after that horrible night when Jacob had been punished for cursing, lying and smoking, he'd told Mark about what had happened. He'd left out the worst parts -- the cigarettes, the spanking, the accusations of lying -- for reasons of embarrassment. But he really did want to introduce Mark to the Masts, so they would know he hadn't been lying about that part, at least.

Of all the transgressions Jacob had committed, and the ones he'd been accused of, he felt as if lying seemed the worst of them. He wanted to clean up his record.

"Oh, good," said Jacob, breathing a sigh of relief. "You exist outside of school."

"Sorry, what?" Mark asked, his eyebrows raised. He hustled across the lawn toward Jacob, nearly bumping into a few older women, who let out exclamations Jacob did not understand.

"You remember," said Jacob, "I told the Masts I was with you that day, and they didn't believe me. So I thought maybe you didn't exist. Ah… it sort of made sense at the time." He shrugged. "What *is* your last name, by the way?"

Mark blinked at him. "Oh, right!" he said, as if remembering. "The cigarettes!"

It was Jacob's turn to stare. "Is there *anything* that *everyone* doesn't know around here?" He was genuinely surprised now, since he knew Thomas had tried to keep the cigarette incident a secret.

"Ah… no," Mark admitted. "No secrets in Hope Crossing, and you live with Sara, who tells all." He gave a slightly embarrassed grin. "Come on, let's go down to the river."

"Before we go, can I introduce you to Mr. Mast?"

Mark looked confused. "He already knows me."

"Yeah, but –"

"Oh, the lying part! Right, okay."

Jacob was really starting to dislike Sara more and more.

"Okay," agreed Mark. "Let's go introduce me. He probably thinks of me as the Beiler boy."

"Beiler boy?"

"Beiler's my last name. Most times adults refer to us as our connection to the family," Mark explained. "*You* are usually referred to as the Mast boy."

"Oh," said Jacob, startled into silence.

They headed towards Mr. Mast, who was talking with some other men from the community. He turned when he saw Jacob and Mark approaching.

Mark smiled at Mr. Mast, pushing his straw hat back on his head. Jacob said, "This is Mark Beiler, the boy I met at school, the day that… well, we hung out together, on… uh, that day. You remember."

Thomas looked confused for a moment. Then the light went on behind his eyes, and he smiled. "Ah, the Beiler boy, Mark. You have befriended Jacob?" he asked.

"Yes, sir." Mark smiled again, friendly and polite, at Thomas and the rest of the men in the group. "I am showing him the Amish way of doing things."

"Good," another man said approvingly. Jacob recognized him by sight, but didn't remember his name. "Where are you boys headed now?"

"To the river, to look around," Mark replied.

"The river?" Jacob asked, but then shut up.

They were waved away by the older men. Together, they walked towards the trees at the edge of the Zooks' field of corn.

"Right, the river. It's like a wide ditch, with water in it, but the water moves. It's amazing, really." Mark laughed at his own joke, and Jacob's rolled eyes made him laugh even more.

"You know, *you* might be a pacifist," Jacob said, following Mark away from the Zooks' home, "but I'm not above hitting you."

"I have about an hour," Mark ignored the mock threat, knowing it was in good fun. "I figured I could get some fishing in."

"How are you going to go fishing without a pole?"

"I keep one by the river. It's a cane pole. Belonged to some guy... Some guy named Jacob, I think." Mark picked up the pace.

Jacob thought about that. "Two questions," he said.

"Let's have 'em."

"First: You stole a fishing pole?"

"Nope. Borrowed, from some guy. He left it there. He's in the *bahn* now." Mark paused. "I sometimes wonder if his fishing pole is in the *bahn,* as well."

"The *bahn*?"

"When someone leaves the community, or is... er... asked to leave, then they're in the *bahn,* or shunned. They can come back if they make a public apology, but we are not allowed to speak to them. We can do business with them, sometimes. Depending on what they've done."

"So I guess my cigarettes don't qualify me for the *'bahn',*" Jacob said. It was a joke, but he actually felt a stirring of anxiety.

"Everyone does stupid things now and then," Mark said. They had reached the river. There was a cobblestone bridge closed by, but not much else in the way of civilization. "It doesn't mean you go to the *bahn*. My older brother, he was caught with a transistor radio, used to keep track of the games. Foozeball, basketball, you know."

Jacob could not be entirely sure, but he wondered if there wasn't a hint of jealousy in Mark's voice. He had never followed sports himself, but he could see how it might have an appeal to someone basically shut off from the rest of the world.

It occurred to him that perhaps Mark was 'hanging out' with him only to learn more about the English world. It didn't seem that farfetched, did it?

"You know to be honest, I never really liked sports," Jacob said apologetically.

"What? I thought that's what the English world was all about." Mark looked incredulous.

"It is for most people, I guess. But I never really had the time." "Well, what did you have time for?"

"Staying alive would be one." Jacob grinned, then laughed. "Plus, at the group home we couldn't really have television or radios. They were afraid someone would steal them from us and cause problems."

"What kind of problems?"

"Well..." Jacob thought. How could he explain his world to Mark? "You know this 'turn the other cheek' stuff you have here? It doesn't really exist in my wor-- in the English world. When someone attacks you, or says something mean to you, you have to fight back."

"Why?"

"Well, if you don't, then you look weak, and it makes other people think you're an easy target. Then instead of having mean things said to you, you end up hurt -- or worse, dead."

"What about the police?"

"We don't trust the police enough to ask them for help. If you call them, then if they need to make a big bust, they might pin something on you -- even hurt you if you try to defend yourself."

"By defend yourself...you mean fight?"

"No, I mean if you try to explain the situation and what went wrong." Jacob sighed. The memories were dark and unpleasant. "They'll hurt you. Or, at least," he added, "they'll hurt people like me. Because to them, I'm lower than dirt."

"I don't understand," Mark said. He had been looking for something in the grass at the edge of the river -- which looked more like a wide creek to Jacob – and now he pulled out the fishing pole. "Aren't all people equal?" he asked Jacob, as he sat down and started baiting the hook.

"I read a book once, a long time ago," Jacob said, recalling the year he'd spent performing community service in the public library. "It said something like... this isn't quite it... but basically: all men are equal, but some men are more equal than others."

"That's a contradiction if I ever heard one." Mark finished baiting the hook, and cast the line into the river.

"I'm having trouble with your world," Jacob confided in him. "First, Dorothy... er, I mean Mrs. Mast... tells me to turn the other cheek. And then when I do it, I get praise. No one comes after me; no one makes fun of me." He shook his head. "I just don't understand how your world works."

"Maybe, just maybe, we've got it figured out. Maybe our world is farther ahead of yours than you think."

"Well..." Jacob began.

He cut himself off, and they both looked up, at the sound of hoof-steps and tires tearing through the grass. What they saw approaching them was possibly the scariest -- yet probably also the funniest -- sight they'd seen in a long time.

It was Deborah Weaver, riding a carriage. But it didn't look like any carriage either of them had seen before. The bottom was there, including the suspension. But the walls were gone, as if they'd been torn off long ago. And instead of the typical buggy seat, something that looked like a park bench had been attached to the floorboards with what seemed to be baling wire and hope.

"Whoa!" Deborah said as draw up to them. The 'buggy' came to a creaking, grinding halt.

Deborah looked down at both of them from the proud height of her vehicle. "Your mother says you need to come home for lunch!"

"Bad luck for you." Jacob grinned at Mark.

"You too," Deborah said, looking sternly at Jacob. "And you are over-due! I should be at home, doing the work of women, but instead here I am chasing the two of you down like loose cattle."

"You could have cut that sentence by half with a contraction here and there," Mark pointed out smugly. "What are you driving, anyway?"

"Oh, this?" Deborah looked at her chariot proudly. "I made it on my own. What do you think?"

"The... er... the question is, what does your father think of it? And is it safe for the road?"

"I was just on the road," Deborah said. She folded her arms and looked down at them regally from her contraption. "And look, I have the flag attached."

She wasn't wrong. She had indeed attached the standard orange "slow vehicle" flag to the back. It seemed to be fastened with the ties from a bread bag.

"Did... did you really *make* this?" Jacob asked warily.

"I did!" Deborah Weaver said, swelling with pride. "It took me months, but I made it!"

"I'm terrified," Jacob said.

"I think I'll walk home," said Mark.

"No, that will never do!" Deborah said. She shook both her finger and her head in their direction. "You have to be home as soon as possible, and I intend to get you there!"

"I think you mean you're trying to take us to heaven, and I ain't ready yet!" Mark dropped his pole, turned around, and started firmly off in the opposite direction.

Deborah looked at Jacob. Jacob simply shrugged. "I'll ride with you," he said.

He walked to the other side of the 'buggy' and climbed up. It wasn't particularly easy, as she had built the thing without a step on either side. In fact, he had to wonder how she'd even managed to climb up into it herself. He imagined her making a running leap, though he realized that was much too silly, even for her.

As soon as he managed to perch himself on the bench, she signaled the horses, and they were headed back toward the road. He briefly wondered how she could even know where the road was. But moments later, they were on it.

This was the very first time he had been alone with Deborah Weaver. He kept stealing glances at her from the side of his vision. He desperately wished for a pair of sunglasses, though nothing of the sort was available out here in Pilgrim-land.

It wasn't easy for him to figure out why he suddenly found himself so attracted to her. It didn't make any sense. She certainly wasn't his type. He was definitely a city boy, and she lived in a deliberately fabricated, old-fashioned countryside hell.

Maybe it was her blonde hair... or could have been, if it weren't tightly wrapped in a bun. Yes, that was certainly it! Or, then again, maybe it was her eyes. He'd read plenty of stories about men losing themselves in the eyes of a beautiful woman. So it didn't seem too much of a stretch.

He had plenty of chances to sneak peeks on the way 'home.' Eventually, of course, she caught him looking, and giggled. She was far better at this than he was.

"You are staring," she said, as the carriage hit a bump and

sent him flying a good eight inches into the air. Apparently, the one thing she'd forgotten to do in creating this thing was attach a good set of shocks.

"Sorry," Jacob said, his cheeks turning red with embarrassment.

She giggled again. That made it worse.

"I had something I wished to ask you," she said, as the 'buggy' neared home... *Jacob* 's home.

"Er..." said Jacob. "Um... okay." Right now he wished for nothing more than to jump out of the buggy and run the rest of the way home.

"There is a volleyball tournament this Saturday, and I would like very much if you would come with me."

"You people play volleyball?" Jacob could hear the disbelief in his own voice. He *was* having trouble believing it.

"Well, of course we do, silly. What else would we do for fun?"

"Well...uh... fish... and... other... stuff?" Jacob suspected he was blushing again.

"It will be this Saturday. Everyone will be there. I will come by your house and pick you up." "In this?" Jacob blurted out.

"Well, I will not be picking you up on foot," Deborah said. "What else would I be using?"

"I don't know," Jacob said, trying to change the subject. "Will the volleyball have air in it?"

CHAPTER SEVEN

The days, then weeks, slipped by. With each one, Jacob became more and more convinced that he wanted to stay in this place.

The outside world, though it had once his home, was beginning to fade, almost as if it had been a bad dream. Here, things that would have sparked massive arguments in the 'real world' would only result in brief discussions. There was always, always enough food. And he simply could not get enough of the night sky. That was a luxury that people in the city could not and never would be able to buy, regardless of their financial status. Even his friend Sherry Thomas was beginning to fade in his mind, replaced by someone new... someone much more important, at least to him.

Rather swiftly, his world had been replaced. It was no longer a stage set lined with broken sidewalks and improperly discarded garbage. Now it was a landscape of sweeping plains, endless fields, and blazing sunsets that bathed everything in an orange light, which, Jacob felt absolutely certain, was what nature had always intended.

Things could only get better from here. At least, that was what Jacob tried to tell himself, though his usual pessimism tended to reassert itself and tell him that his life had simply reached its highest point, and would now inevitably go downhill.

"Pass the potatoes," Thomas said from the end of the massive table.

Before the sentence had even been finished, Deborah was pushing the mashed potato bowl across the table, toward him.

Dinner at the Mast house was not so different from dinner at the group home, at least as far as the food was concerned. Tonight the menu consisted of mashed potatoes, gravy, pork chops, and green beans, in massive quantities. The biggest difference here, however, was that there was always food enough for everyone.

"Jacob," Thomas said. "Did you feed the hogs this morning?

They're being a little noisy."

"Yes sir," Jacob replied. "But the one in the middle, she keeps knocking her bowl over. It's getting old."

Thomas nodded, deep in thought.

"I should get a heavier bowl," he concluded.

"It's rubber," Jacob said, taking a bite out of his pork chop. "I nailed it to the wall."

"Or that," Thomas said.

"You should see what Jacob did in school today!" said Sara.

"That sounds interesting," said Dorothy. "But maybe Jacob should tell us, if it's his story."

Jacob glanced across the table and saw that Sara was practically shaking, dying to get the story out. It wasn't a big deal to him, but he was glad that Sara had warmed up to him recently.

"Go ahead," he said to her.

"He taught Jimmy Byler how to read!" She sounded so impressed that Jacob felt obliged to explain. "It wasn't that hard."

"The Byler boy doesn't talk," Dorothy said. Her question indicated curiosity, though her tone remained calm.

"But now he reads," Jacob said.

"Interesting," Thomas said, thoughtfully.

After a few moments, he rose from the table, and exited the kitchen through the back door. Jacob excused himself as well, and set off walking toward the back of the property, as he had been doing every night.

He supposed that Thomas, Mark and – well – everyone else

in the community were used to the way the landscape looked at night. It probably didn't seem interesting to them at all. But Jacob simply could not get enough of it.

There had been a time when he'd believed that everything would simply be pitch black at night without the aid of streetlights. It continued to amaze him, night after night, that the moon and stars could be so bright.

He came across the tree where he'd once buried the pack of cigarettes (not so long ago… forever ago), and sat down, facing the woods.

Sometimes, if he closed his eyes, he could almost hear the sound of the river in the distance: the river, and all its tributaries, running like veins through the countryside, providing the life-giving water that Hope Crossing relied on.

He remembered lying in his bed, deep in the city, far away from Hope Crossing. Outside the window, he had always been able to hear cars, the unending traffic coming and going. The honking of horns, police sirens, shouting, even the occasional gunshot.

Here the air was clear, and the night so was silent that, if you listened closely, you might be able to hear the sound of animals moving through the forest, making their last journey before settling in for the night.

Then there was the sky. That beautiful canvas, glowing brilliantly in the dead of the night, and the stars, all of which would vanish by the time morning came. He had seen it before -- in fact, he'd once spent the night in the backyard, watching (oddly enough no one had seemed to care) -- but he found he simply couldn't get enough of it. Even now, he was curious about those stars that the night sky left behind when it finally transitioned to the pale blue of morning.

Settling down on his back under the tree, he thought he felt a bump beneath him. It was something solid -- probably a rock. He reached beneath himself, grasped it, and pulled it out to have a look. Of all things, it was the lighter from his cigarette pack. It must have fallen out of the pack. He tucked it in his pocket; he would throw it away later.

Maybe he would sleep out here again. Since he'd started discovering the wonders nature had to offer, Jacob hadn't had much interest in spending time indoors. He closed his eyes – it had been a long day – and, gradually, started to drift off.

But his slumber was interrupted by what he thought was yelling. He immediately opened his eyes, sat up, and looked about.

He was a fair distance away from the Mast house. But he could make out the shapes of Thomas, Dorothy, and Sara running out the back door toward the buggy. (Did they ever use the front door for anything?) For a moment, he thought of calling out to them, but he was at least half a mile out. So, instead, he simply watched as the buggy pulled out of the driveway and took a right turn, toward town.

He got up, and followed as quickly as he could on foot.

He knew he would lose sight of the buggy one way or another, and, sure enough, that happened soon. But there was only one way they could have gone, so he didn't have to worry about losing them.

Jacob covered the first half-mile at a run easily enough, but as he passed the Mast residence, he started to run out of breath. He stopped for a moment, doubled over, heaving in air, and then resumed running.

It was a good five minutes, maybe more, before he saw smoke on the horizon, glowing ominously in a yellow-reddish light. Of course, Jacob had seen smoke before; there were plenty of industrial parks in the city. But way out here, it had to be a house fire or a barn. He took off running again, toward the smoke.

***

As he finally approached the fire, he could plainly see it was indeed a building. Not a house, but a barn. A huge barn, much larger than the Masts', stood engulfed in flames. It was already surrounded by people. They had formed several assembly lines, working to pass buckets filled with water.

They had responded quickly, but it was far too late. Jacob watched the devastation as the structure burned to the ground. In just a matter of minutes, it was reduced to a shadow of its former glory. The flames eventually burned down where they stood. The volunteers were able to keep them from spreading beyond the site, but there was nothing left of the barn but a few burning embers, and a group of extremely disappointed and forlorn people.

For a few moments, there was dead silence. But it was quickly broken by a loud, booming voice.

"Who did this?" shouted a man. "Did anyone see anything?" "Daed, it was probably an accident!" Jacob recognized Deborah Weaver's voice, and saw her stepping out from the crowd. So, this angry farmer must be her father.

"Barns don't catch fire without a reason!" Mr. Weaver said. He threw his arms up, and walked toward the plume of smoke. "My grandfather built that barn with his two hands. I'm gonna--"

He stopped suddenly. Jacob was standing some way back from the crowd, but he realized that Mr. Weaver had spotted him, and was staring straight at him.

"You!" the farmer shouted, his voice full of venom. "I know you! You're the outsider! You did this!"

"Hold on!" Jacob said. "I just got here! I ran here from the Masts' --"

"Now," Thomas said, "there's no need to go accusin' anyone.

This is a big deal. We need to be careful."

"Empty your pockets, boy," Mr. Weaver said. He stepped forward, looming threateningly, almost as if he were ready to choke the life out of Jacob. "If ye ain't got nothing to hide, then empty your pockets and let it show!"

"You know what? Fine," Jacob said. He could feel the eyes of the entire town upon him. "Just to show you I've got nothing to hide--"

He reached into his pockets.

And a lump formed in his throat, as he felt, and suddenly remembered, the one and only thing he'd put in them today. The one thing that really, really didn't need to be there.

The cigarette lighter.

"Well?" Mr. Weaver said, holding out his arms. "The world is waitin'! Let's see whatcha got in there!"

Jacob closed his eyes as his stomach began to clench.

Maybe he could explain. Maybe Thomas would be able to help him out. Maybe….

He pulled the lighter out of his pocket. His fist was clenched, and he knew his face must be white as a sheet.

"What's that in your hand, boy?" Mr. Weaver demanded. "Open it up, let me see."

He opened his hand slowly. In it lay the orange BIC lighter.

Mr. Weaver stood silent for a moment. Then he took a single

step away. He folded his arms, and stood up straight.

"Stay away from my property. And stay away from my daughter."

He turned to walk away. Around them, with a slow sound of moving feet, like water moving in the tide, everyone around them did the same. Except for the Mast family.

Jacob stood, about fifteen feet away, staring at the Masts. They stared back at him, as if he were the scourge of the earth.

"I didn't do it," Jacob said. He knew he sounded defiant. He also knew that, judging from his experience, it wasn't likely to make a single lick of difference.

He'd been accused of many things in the past. Some he had done; some he hadn't done. But it never made a difference. In all cases, one person would play judge, jury, and executioner – and this one would be just the same.

Nonetheless, he couldn't help but try to defend himself. "Why would I do it? Burn down a barn? Think about it! It doesn't make sense! None of this makes sense!"

But Thomas and the rest of the family maintained their distance. They didn't move; they refused to speak.

"Say something!" Jacob shouted. "Come on -- you have to say *something*!"

They didn't.

Instead, they turned, as one, without a word, and headed back toward the buggy.

Jacob was left all alone in the field.

He dropped to his knees. And he came close – he didn't quite do it, but he came very close -- to burying his head in the dirt, as the Mast family climbed into their buggy, and drove off.

***

It took a lot longer to walk back to the house than it had taken to run from it. And when he arrived, it appeared to be empty.

This, of course, was impossible, since the buggy was parked in the back. Still, the house seemed deserted. He called out, trying to get a response from someone.

"Hello?" He stepped over the threshold of the front door and stopped. "Is anyone home?"

No answer, just his voice echoing off the hardwood floors and nearly bare walls. Not even a single lamp was burning on the hallway table, as it usually was.

Something was terribly wrong.

He continued down the hallway, and came to the stairwell on the left side of the hall, just in front of the door that led to what Jacob had always assumed to be a laundry room. He peeked through the cracked-open door, and saw no one. Heading up the stairs, things were no different. He called out again, and then again, and then he found that all of the doors upstairs, save for his, were closed.

"Anyone up here?" he called out. No response. None whatsoever.

He continued down the hall to his room, stepped through the door and paused.

Though he had not gathered much in the way of personal effects over the past few weeks, the space was unusually bare. The window he had shut before leaving was now standing wide open, as if the room were airing out. Even the bed was made.

The most disturbing thing, however, was his bag, packed and ready to go, sitting at the edge of his bed. All of his belongings had been removed from their places around the room and placed neatly into the bag.

They were going to send him off without so much as a goodbye. (Well, then again, he probably deserved it.)

But what the heck was he supposed to do now? Go live in the forests?

Though, at the moment, that didn't sound like a half-bad idea...

He picked the bag up for a moment, and then dropped it to the floor again. He walked out into the hallway -- the rest of the doors were still shut – and stood still for a moment. Then he began to speak, although he had no idea as to whether or not anyone was actually listening.

"Look, I didn't do it," he said angrily. "Why the hell would I go and ruin everything like that?" He paused. "I know you've already made up your mind. Everyone always does. But did it ever cross your simple minds that maybe, just maybe, you're *wrong?*"

The thinly veiled insult, which he'd hoped would draw at least one of them out, had no effect whatsoever, and Jacob felt his last hope fade.

He stomped his foot angrily. The sound reverberated through the entire second floor. Then he walked back into his 'room', and plopped down onto the bed. This had been his one chance, and he'd blown it. Even if he hadn't meant to.

Really, how much more stupid could he possibly have been? If he'd been near the house in the first place, they would have simply taken him with them. And maybe, if he'd really been thinking, he wouldn't have taken a lighter to a barn fire!

He shook his head. Where was he going to go from here? His anger was doing a great job of blocking his higher brain functions.

He wasn't sure how long he sat there. Was it an hour? Even more? In the daze of despair and physical exhaustion he was in, he thought he even dozed off for a while.

Finally, after what felt like hours, he sat up on the bed with a jerk. He hopped to his feet, grabbed his bag, and headed for the stairs.

It was time to get out of here – even if he still wasn't sure where he was going. With any luck, though, he could hitch a ride out of town, maybe to New Jersey, or New York, or one of those other states that started with 'New.'

Closing the front door behind him, and turning to scan the porch, he beheld the most unusual sight he'd seen in days: a car rolling down the driveway.

"What the..." he muttered as he watched it draw closer and closer.

It was an old, beat-up Cavalier. Almost like...

"No way!"

It was Carol. She must have driven all the way from the city.

"Get in," she said through the open driver-side window.

Jacob took one last look back at the house. Then he sighed and climbed into the vehicle. He tossed his bag into the back seat.

"Less than six months," she said as, she turned the car around and sped up the driveway, toward the road. "Seriously -- less than one month." He saw her shake her head. "I can't do anything more for you, Jacob. You can spend the night at the home, and then... well, I guess you'll stay at the county jail for a while. There is good news there, though: once they find something to convict you of, you'll get three square meals a day and a nice ...cot to sleep on."

"Great," Jacob said. He pressed his head to the passenger side window, and watched the moonlit farms, hills, and silos of Hope Crossing disappear from his sight forever. "Would it do any good to say that I didn't do it?" He stared at the side of Carol's head. Her gaze was intent on the road ahead. "No, I guess it wouldn't."

A tear ran down his cheek. He brushed it away quickly. Another slid down the opposite cheek. This one, he didn't even bother to wipe away.

Carol spoke softly, almost whispering. "Maybe we can sort things out, when the smoke clears. But... I need the truth, Jacob."

"What good is the truth?" he said bitterly. "Nobody believes me anyway. Might as well just cop to it, and you can lock me up until I'm 18. Then I can blow this town, and this whole messed-up system. And nobody will be able to stop me."

He heard Carol sigh, but he didn't care.

What made everything worse was that the Masts had acted as if they actually liked him. If only he could prove his innocence! But that seemed unlikely.

He wished he could, though. He wished he could go back and prove his innocence to them, and then he'd tell them where they could go, with all their high and mighty "ways of the Lord." Forgiveness and truth? What a joke.

What was it that preacher had always liked to say?

"'God is spirit, and those who worship Him must worship in spirit and truth.' "

Yeah, right, he thought. We can see how well that worked out for me.

CHAPTER EIGHT

"Welcome back," Charles said as Jacob walked into the room.

Apparently, his old bed still had not been claimed by anyone else.

"Go to hell," Jacob said wearily. He collapsed onto the bed, covering his face with both hands.

"Hey," Charles said, "don't worry. Word has it they're sending a van out tomorrow to take you to county. It's not so bad. I have a few friends there I can hook you up with."

"You realize the next step after county is juvie, right? You got any friends over there?"

"Never made it that far," Charles said.

Jacob groaned.

Charles grinned, reached under his bed, and pulled out his contraband Gameboy. Jacob watched idly. "What's on the menu tonight?" he asked. Just like old times.

"Pokémon Yellow." Charles flipped the device on.

"Didn't you beat that one already?" Jacob asked.

"Does it look like I'm made of money?" Charles demanded. "Yeah, I hear they have Pokémon Emerald now, and Leaf Green, and all that crap. But I'm stuck here with a Gameboy that was made in..."

He flipped the Gameboy over to check the manufacture date.

"… Wow. 1995."

"And, what do you know, it still works." Jacob turned to face the wall as the inevitable clicking and clacking of buttons commenced.

"Lights out!" a voice shouted from the hallway. "Lights out now!"

"You can't play in the dark," Jacob said, almost concerned.

"I'll just hold a flashlight in my mouth," Charles muttered. He reached over and switched the room light off.

The second he did, it went pitch black – for a moment. Then Jacob's eyes adjusted to the change, courtesy of the glaring streetlamp outside.

In Hope Crossing, it would have been the moon that provided the light. And not quite as violently.

"Crap," Jacob said, pulling the old, ratty pillow over his head.

"What?"

"Um," said Jacob. He didn't want to be caught being mopey. "That light..."

"Same light as every night," said Charles. "Did you forget about it so quickly?" He sounded mildly curious. "Want me to knock it out again?"

"Could you?" Jacob asked.

But Charles said, "I'll get around to it." He was clearly lost in his game, and no longer in the mood to pay attention to... much of anything.

Jacob sat up suddenly. "I've gotta go," he said, hopping off the bed and heading toward the door.

Charles said nothing. Jacob cracked the door and stepped out into the hallway, pulling the door shut behind him.

On most nights, there was at least one person patrolling the halls, though they spent the majority of their time watching TV in the downstairs lobby. He held still for a moment, and listened. He could definitely hear the sound of a television blaring downstairs. (Whoever it was watching *Seinfeld*. He'd always hated that show -- though he'd found that sitting in front of it for too long would cause you to become mysteriously glued to your seat.)

He turned left and headed for the staircase at the end of the hall, though he wasn't quite sure what he was looking for. The moment he entered the stairwell, however, he realized who he'd been looking for, because he found her there, looking for him. Of course: Sherry Thomas.

"I was just coming to see you," she said. "I heard they sent you to… well, to hell."

They sat down in the staircase. Probably it was the safest place in the group home, at least at night. No one was likely to wander in here – no one except for them.

He told her everything, or almost everything. He was thoughtful enough to omit the part about Deborah Weaver, although, he thought, it didn't really matter. He wasn't ever going to be seeing Deborah again.

"Okay," Sherry said. She brushed her long red hair out of her face. "You know, Jacob, I've known you for a long, long time. I mean, ever since we stole that Gameboy for Charles and--"

"He needs a new one."

"Really? Already? Anyway, I've known you for a long time. And when you want something, you don't just give up. You always try -- even if you fail."

"There's no point here," Jacob argued. "They hate me. They think—"

"Right, they think you burned their barn down. Did you? By the way?"

"What? No! I didn't burn down their barn! And I want to prove it to them. I really wanna prove it, before they send me to County." Jacob was getting worked up. "Not so they don't send me to jail; I don't even care about that anymore. I just want to see the look on their faces, when they find out they condemned me without proof. I want them to know that I gave their way of life a try, and when it really came down to it, all those Scriptures they teach day in and day out don't amount to diddly squat, because they don't practice what they preach. They packed me up so fast and kicked me out so hard, I didn't even get to say goodbye to them. … Not that I care," he added, a little unconvincingly.

"Wow! These people really got to you." Sherry smiled slightly. "You must have really like it there."

"No. Of course not. I was just marking time until I could get out of there."

Sherry was still smiling. Her green-eyed gaze twinkled in the slight light. "Yeah? Remember who you're talking to, Jacob."

Jacob felt a warm heat rising up his neck into his ears. Sherry always had always one to cut to the point. "I guess I was getting used to being there," he admitted grudgingly. "And, Dorothy did make great food."

Sherry didn't press, but she did change the subject -- to something less touchy-feely, Jacob noticed, and more practical.

"All right," she said. "Here's what we're going to do. We're going to get you back there, and this time, you're going to stay there."

Jacob blinked at her. She sounded confident, but he didn't dare to hope. "I thought *I* was the dreamer," he said.

"Well," said Sherry, "you said these people are religious, right?"

"Right. And I know that's not your thing -- but it was amazing, seriously! For a few weeks I had a family...and my own room. Can you imagine that? My own room! And home-cooked meals!"

"I've had my own room here for years," Sherry pointed out. "No one else is allowed to bunk with me."

"Oh, right," Jacob said. "The… eh, the...smell… thing."

"I'm going to kill you if you bring that up again, but seriously, have you ever heard the story of David? You can use that to your advantage."

"You want me to kill Thomas with a rock?"

"Do you think that would help? No, but really -- let me tell you a story..."

***

"I'm not sure this is safe," Jacob said. He was standing on the edge of the roof, staring down at the streets below.

"*This* is a fire escape," Sherry said. "What's not really safe is walking two hundred miles."

"I don't actually trust this fire escape," Jacob said, looking down at the rickety old staircase. He felt pretty certain that this had been a three-floor paper factory at one time, before being converted into a group home -- though Carol adamantly denied it. It would only make sense, of course, with the mismatched architecture *inside* the building.

Sherry ignored him. "I've packed a bag for you," she went on. "You've got a loaf of bread, peanut butter and jelly, a little box of cereal, and, most importantly, a bottle of water."

"Right... the most important thing," he repeated back to her. "And Hope Crossing is which way?"

"East." He repeated what she'd told him earlier. "Hope Crossing is to the east."

She handed him a small pocket compass. "I stole it from the janitor. He won't miss it for a few days, I suspect. It was under a pile of junk. Anyway, all you really need to do is keep walking, and you'll get there one way or another."

"Great," said Jacob, as he carefully stepped out on to the fire escape.

"Oh, Jacob -- one more thing." She leaned over, and planted a kiss directly on his lips. "*That's* how you do it."

Then she was gone, back through the door, presumably to her room. Jacob stood there for a moment, stunned, and then proceeded down the fire escape.

CHAPTER NINE

The trip to Hope Crossing, originally, had taken just under four hours at 242 miles. On foot, by Jacob's estimation, it would take about eighty hours, accounting for distractions, food stops and physical incapability.

Physical incapability, of course, was something that Jacob was experiencing at this very moment.

He had found a way outside the city limits not long ago, though it had been much harder than he'd imagined. In fact, it was just about twenty-four hours ago that he'd stood before a huge drainage pipe, just large enough for him to walk through, so long as he kept his head down and nose closed.

The pipe had eventually led to a freeway, which he had been forced to cross. From his previous experience, he felt pretty sure that his hop, skip, and jump across that freeway had prompted someone to call the police, and that certainty pressed him to hasten his nocturnal journey across the countryside. He didn't *think* that they would pull out the helicopters and the search lights for him, but you could never be sure.

Now here he sat, a good twenty miles outside of the city, resting in a patch of forest. His legs were already ruined for the day. Each time he'd tried to resume walking, his leg muscles contracted painfully. In fact, he was forced to sit with his legs extended out straight, to try to avoid the muscle contractions.

This was more than a bit inconvenient, since he had a long way yet to go. He sat there, waiting for the muscle contractions to stop, and massaging his thighs and calves to try to coax them into working again. Finally, when he felt as if we couldn't wait any longer, he pulled himself back up onto wobbly legs, and took up again his long walk back toward Hope Crossing.

The walk was much harder than he'd imagined. The ground was horribly uneven, and his shoes -- tennis shoes he'd received from the shelter last year -- weren't holding up to the job. The sidewall of one of his sneakers had already torn, leaving the side of his foot exposed to the elements. He'd stepped through a few water puddles, and his socks were soaked. On top of that, his feet were freezing. He was able to walk for what he estimated to be ten minutes at a time before collapsing onto the earth, and waiting until his muscles would cooperate again.

He wasn't sure how long he went on like this -- walking in ever-shorter spurts -- but eventually he was forced to stop and actually rest.

As he curled up beneath a tree, he remembered his first morning on Thomas's farm, and how his body had ached. That first morning was nothing compared to what he felt now. It was no wonder that people had invented cars!

He slept for a few hours, and then set off again. He knew that he still had to be a long way – days? – from Hope Crossing, but he still felt convinced that any moment, he would see it off in the distance. Of course, that didn't happen.

He collapsed once again into the grass, and opened the bag Sherry had packed for him. The bread was almost gone, but there was still a fair amount of jelly and peanut butter. The water, however was nearly gone, and he'd yet to come across a stream, lake, or river to refill it. He nearly hurled the bottle away in anger, but then thought better of it.

He zipped the bag shut again, and continued once more on his journey, which was starting to feel more and more doomed.

He wondered how long he'd managed to walk so far. Thirty miles? Surely not even half the trip, yet.

As he pulled himself through a cornfield, half-expecting to fall over dead at any moment, he contemplated just how stupid this endeavor had been. Back in the city, it had seemed like an outstanding idea. But now that he was out here, he realized that there was no food, no shelter, and nowhere to go for help. How dense could he have been?

He'd stopped for a moment to rest, again, when he spotted a figure approaching across the field -- presumably from the road.

The road! Of course, he thought – he could just head for the road, and stick his thumb out. It might not be exactly safe, but at this point he didn't think his odds of making it the rest of the way on foot were too good either.

He began to walk in that direction, across the field, hoping to pass the mysterious figure, or at least ignore it.

But as he did, he couldn't help but notice that the figure kept coming toward him. It seemed to be making a beeline for him, no matter how he turned.

What should he do? His impulse was to run. But, exhausted and barely able to move his legs, he was in no condition right now to escape anyone. Finally, he just gave up and stood still, waiting for the man to reach him. If he was doomed, he figured, then he was doomed.

The man was almost close enough to make out. Taller and taller… in fact, he was unusually tall…

Jacob saw, to his shock, that it was Thomas.

"What the *hell*?" he croaked. His voice cracked. He hadn't used it in hours. Since yesterday?

"I don't believe this," Thomas said. He was staring at Jacob as if he were a ghost or a runaway horse, and, for once, ignored Jacob's swearing. "Carol told me you took off," he said, "and that you might be coming back to my house. But I didn't believe you'd actually try it." He shook his massive head, slowly.

"She said you still say you're innocent," he added.

Jacob was spurred to action. After all, this was what he'd come all this way for. He pointed at Thomas, still breathing heavily, but he forced out his voice. "You need to hear me out."

"Well," Thomas said, "I suppose I'd better. Since you came all this way -- I reckon close to forty miles, on foot!"

"I didn't burn down that barn!" said Jacob. He had to tell Thomas this, make sure he heard him. "You *know* I didn't burn down that barn," he added. "But you sent me back to the city to rot in jail."

"I *don't* know that you didn't burn down that barn," Thomas replied. "I came out here because Dorothy wouldn't leave me be until I came and collected you." he shook his head again. "I'm going to take you back there myself right now. You are a liability. Do you know what that means?" Jacob did, and it hurt, but Thomas went on anyway. "It means we cannot trust you. Plain and simple."

Time for Plan B. Jacob unzipped his bag. He reached into the bottom, as quickly as he could with his chilled and aching hands, and pulled out the one other thing Sherry had given him before he'd left.

It was a Bible.

Jacob held it out partway toward Thomas. "This book says God forgives," he said. "Are *you* better than God?"

Thomas sighed. "I can forgive you," he said. "But I can't give you a second chance. There's a big difference."

"What about David?" Jacob demanded.

Thomas looked at him in surprise now. He raised an eyebrow. "What do you mean, what about David?"

"God did more than forgive him," Jacob said. Sherry had rehearsed this with him; they'd both figured that Jacob would only get one chance. And that chance was now.

"He gave David a second chance to be king," Jacob went on. "You know what David did! He sent his best friend to die on the front line so he could be with his wife, *and* cover up her pregnancy. God *knows* he did that! And he let him stay, anyway. Now," he said, still holding out the Bible, challengingly. "What do you *know* that I did?"

Thomas thought for a moment. "Well... I don't know, for sure, that you started that barn fire. That is true." He rubbed his beard thoughtfully. "I made have made a mistake, in haste." Jacob held his breath.

"You are the only outsider in our community," Thomas went on, as if talking to himself. He seemed to be weighing up the pros and cons. "However, Dorothy was none too happy about packing you off back to the city. You have made quite an impression on my wife, and, when she heard you'd vanished again, I didn't hear the end of it until I agreed to come and try to find you."

"That barn fire could have been an accident. You didn't even give me a chance. Why didn't you just spank me like before?" Jacob asked. "You just packed up my bags for me, and called Carol. Do you know how I felt?"

"It's not going to be easy." Thomas sidestepped the accusation. "The Weavers hate you now. And you can't be around their girl anymore." It seemed he wasn't going to answer Jacob's question. But that was all right, because, from the way he was talking, Jacob was starting to have hope again.

"We may have to talk to the Bishop about setting things right," Thomas said. "You know, her father, Caleb, was going to do some work on my house. And now I'll have to do it myself."

"So, I'll help you," Jacob said. "And maybe we can patch things up later. The truth will come out. I know it will. Because it wasn't me."

"I'm beginning to think you're telling the truth,"

Thomas said. Jacob felt his heart swell with joy. Thomas believed him!

Thomas gestured for Jacob to follow him. He picked up Jacob's bag, and they turned and headed back to the road from which Thomas had come.

Waiting on the road was an old brown-and-white station wagon.

"I thought --" Jacob began. Then he stopped when he spotted another man behind the wheel. "Oh," he said, "you got a driver."

Thomas nodded. "We have been looking for you for quite a while. Get in the back." He walked around the station wagon and climbed into the front, on the passenger side.

"Is this your boy?" the man asked, and Thomas nodded in the affirmative.

"Your boy." Jacob leaned back into the worn seat, suddenly very tired. He liked this car, he decided. It reminded him of the car from those old reruns of *The Brady Bunch.* Not that he would ever have admitted he liked that show, of course… six kids, a mom and dad, stupid problems, and lots of love…

He was getting sleepy.

Thomas looked back at him. "I don't know for sure if we can fix things," he said soberly. "But I'll do my best not to leave you behind again."

Jacob mustered up enough energy for a reply. It came out kind of poetic, maybe because he was ready to pass out. "There's nothing wrong with being left behind sometimes," he said. "The sky leaves behind a few stars every morning, and usually, what the sky leaves behind shines the brightest."

Thomas regarded him with a shade of surprised humor gracing his face. His eyebrows were raised, and a slight smile was on his lips. "Humility, boy," he said, but his voice was gentle. "Humility."

Then he turned back. Jacob overheard him start talking to the driver – Zach, he called him – about the ordinary, dull details of life in Amish country: crops, weather, horses, baking, wives, daughters, and sons.

Jacob thought he had never been so glad to hear it.

He thought about those Whoopie pies he had eaten; the shoofly pie Dorothy made; those delicious molasses cookies Sara had given him. He was heading back to all of that.

It wasn't perfect. Life was never perfect. The

community still suspected him, and Deborah would be off limits until he had proven his innocence…

But at least for now, he was headed back to the Amish family that had taken him in. For now, he decided as he nodded off to sleep to the gentle rolling of the car's wheels. That was enough.

THE END.

THANK YOU FOR READING!

And thank you for supporting me as an independent author. I hope you enjoyed reading this as much as I enjoyed writing it! If so, I hope you also enjoy the sample of the next book in the series, A LANCASTER AMISH PRAYER FOR JACOB, in the next chapter.

Also, if you get a chance to leave me a review, I'd really appreciate it (and if you find something in the book that – YIKES – makes you think it deserves less than 5-stars, drop me a line at Rachel.stoltzfus@globagrafxpress.com, and I'll fix it if I can)

All the best,

Rachel

A PRAYER FOR JACOB

CHAPTER ONE

"What's the point of all this anyway?" Jacob asked as Thomas once again took control of the plow and straightened it. He didn't have a watch, or any way to tell the time, but they had been out here in the field since early morning, and it had only become hotter. Jacob actually began to feel as if he were standing in an oven, and he was none too happy about it. In fact, he was beginning to question whether he belonged out here at all. He tried to think of what he would be doing right now if he were back in the city. It was a Saturday, so probably nothing at all! Wouldn't that be nice? In fact, he probably would have just been waking up. Of course that was wishful thinking. He would wind up in juvenile hall, or somewhere equally unappealing.

"I told you, we plow the field, then we plant," Thomas said not terribly irritated by Jacob's repeated questions.

"But why?" Jacob asked again. "Can't we just dig some holes in the ground and plant the seeds?" He told Thomas about an old school project where they had poured potting soil into a Styrofoam cup and watched a bean sprout grow. What he failed to mention is that the bean sprout died about a week later.

"The field must be fertilized and plowed, and it must be done properly," Thomas said after listening to Jacob's tale. "This is not a cup; it's a field." He ordered the horse to begin moving again. It did so almost reluctantly. Jacob watched as it put one foot in front of the other and made its way across the terrain finally regaining a steady pace. It wasn't even their field. Their neighbor, Mr. Wendell, had fallen ill recently, and as a result, the care of his fields had fallen by the wayside. Jacob had no idea why Thomas was so willing to help, but he was sure there would be no return on this physical investment.

In other words, this was an act of charity. Thomas had quoted a Bible verse to that effect when Jacob had pestered him on the point that he had to memorize as they worked: *2 Corinthians 9:7, Each man should give what he has decided in his heart to give, not reluctantly or under compulsion, for God loves a cheerful giver.* He knew that Thomas would ask him about it later.

"Isn't the stuff going to grow no matter what?" Jacob asked again.

Thomas sighed and signaled for the horse to stop once again. "Listen to me," Thomas said, "when we fertilize the fields we introduce nutrients into the soil, and those nutrients help the crops to grow. Yes, sure, them crops might grow just fine without those nutrients, but that doesn't mean we should let them grow on their own. Just like in life, the way you turn out depends on the things and people you have around you. It changes your outlook on life, as you'd expect, and overall, you wouldn't be none too happy."

"Are you seriously using me as an example for planting the fields?"

"Well let's face it, you wouldn't have done too well in that shelter would you? In a way, moving you out here is like transplanting you to a more fertile field."

Jacob fell silent thinking as Thomas started the horse up again. Wiping the sweat from his brow and glancing at his mud covered boots. he was reminded of the massive flat snow shoes he'd seen on television shows about the arctic. Television. That was definitely something he missed. Fertile ground. This could be considered that. It had just never been explained to him like that before.

"Now take this for a minute would you?" Thomas said, handing the plow over to Jacob.

Jacob grabbed the massive handles and tried to hold the wooden assembly straight as the horse pulled it through the changing terrain. More often than not, he found himself lifting his feet to knee height, and he quickly became exhausted. "You see, to make positive change, we have to do what we have to do – even if it involves walking through the mud. You see what I'm saying?"

"I hear you talking a lot," Jacob grumped not willing to admit he got the point just yet. "Whatever point you're trying to make, this isn't really the time."

Thomas laughed that large grin he had when he knew Jacob knew what he was talking about, but wasn't ready to give in just yet. "Proverbs 11:2: When pride comes, then comes disgrace, but with humility comes wisdom."

Jacob felt like saying more; he was exhausted and only half the day was gone. They had started in the wee hours of the morning, and had, at this point, managed to plow about half the field.

Though he would never admit it, Jacob was more than a little impressed at Thomas's ability to hold the plow steady. Each time Jacob had taken it, the 'machine' had veered off course going to the left or to the right, causing the field to become what appeared to be a modern art masterpiece. He sighed as they continued pushing the stupid thing through the dirt, more than ready to be finished with the whole exercise.

"Look," he said, "we don't need to complete this entire field today, do we?"

THANK YOU FOR READING!

And thank you for supporting me as an independent author. I hope you enjoyed reading this as much as I loved writing it!

If so, look for this book in eBook or Paperback format at your favorite online book distributors. Also, when a series is complete, or when a series has a significant number of books, we usually put out a discounted collection. If you'd rather read the entire series at once and save a few bucks doing it, we recommend looking for the collection.

Lastly, if you enjoyed this boxed set and want to continue to support my writing, please leave me a review to let everyone know what you thought of the series. It's the best thing you can do to keep indie authors like me writing. (And if you find something in the book that – YIKES – makes you think it deserves less than 5-stars, drop me a line at Rachel.stoltzfus@globagrafxpress.com, and I'll fix it if I can.)

All the best,

Rachel

ABOUT THE AUTHOR

Rachel was born and raised in Lancaster, Pennsylvania. Being a neighbor of the Mennonite community, she started writing Amish romance fiction as a way of looking at the Amish community. She wanted to present a fair and honest representation of a love that is both romantic and sweet. She hopes her readers enjoy her efforts.

CPSIA information can be obtained
at www.ICGtesting.com
Printed in the USA
LVHW02s1827150518
577262LV00015B/1202/P

9 781523 399406